THE SECRET OF
SECCO CANYON

BY

PATRICIA MATTHEWS

READING LEVEL 4

CB

CONTEMPORARY BOOKS

a division of NTC/CONTEMPORARY PUBLISHING GROUP
Lincolnwood, Illinois USA

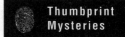

Thumbprint
Mysteries

MORE THUMBPRINT MYSTERIES

by Patricia Matthews:

Dead Man Riding
Death in the Desert

This is a work of fiction. The characters, incidents, and dialogues are products of the author's imagination and are not to be construed as real. Any resemblance to actual events or persons, living or dead, is entirely coincidental.

Cover Design: Matt Zumbo

ISBN: 0-8092-0606-4

Published by Contemporary Books,
a division of NTC/Contemporary Publishing Group, Inc.,
4255 West Touhy Avenue,
Lincolnwood (Chicago), Illinois 60646-1975 U.S.A.
Manufactured in the United States of America.

890 QB 0987654321

CHAPTER 1

"This must be the spot," Rob Harding said aloud to himself.

He pulled the pickup off onto the turnout, parked, and got out. He walked over to the guardrail and looked down into the broad valley below.

The ranch was larger than he had imagined. The main ranch house was big and sprawling. There were a number of other buildings around it. Further away from the house were holding pens for horses and cattle.

The land looked dry. Grass was scarce. In back of the ranch, giant pillars of red rock stood tall against the bright blue of the sky. But it wasn't all dry and bare. Surrounding the ranch buildings were tall, green shade trees. There was also an orchard. The trees were trimmed and set in orderly rows. There was a large pond next to the orchard.

When Rob was told about the ranch, he had asked why it was called Shadow Ranch. He had been told that the name came from the tall, red pillar of rock to the west. The shadow of the rock fell on the ranch house late in the afternoon.

Rob could see men working on the fences. In the distance, he could see two other men on horseback. They were riding away from the ranch.

He stood looking at the ranch for a long time. He realized that he was putting off the moment when he would have to go down there. When he did, he would have to become someone else. Someone named Bobby Tyrell. He would have to lie to the men he would be working with. He would also have to watch his back. From now on, that would be a fact of life. It came with the job. He had some misgivings about this undercover business. Still, sometimes that was the only way to break a case. And that's what it was all about.

He was satisfied with his first look at Shadow Ranch. Rob got back into his pickup and drove on.

When Rob drove up before the ranch house and parked, it was the noon hour. Several men were eating lunch. They sat at a table beneath a large oak tree at one side of the house. They were dressed in jeans, faded work shirts, boots, and Stetson hats.

Rob got out of the pickup and started to walk over to them. They all stopped eating and looked at him curiously. Because of his cover, he was wearing "city" clothes. He was without a hat, and he wore a bright, short-sleeved shirt over a pair of new jeans. Instead of cowboy boots he wore a pair of stained sneakers. He knew he looked out of place.

Rob knew what they saw when they looked at him. They saw a tall, muscular man in his early thirties. His thick, black hair was worn long. His eyes were dark and usually solemn. A rather large nose dominated his long face. His skin was light brown in color. Women had told him he was handsome, that he had a good face. He hoped they were right.

He came closer to the table. Now he saw that two of the men appeared to be American Indians. One was older by some twenty years. He looked at Rob with expressionless, black eyes. The younger one gave Rob a friendly nod.

Rob said, "I'm looking for a Mr. John Mackey."

The man who had given him a friendly nod said, "Mr. Mackey is in the main house. Go down the west side of the house. He has an office there. Knock on the first door."

Rob said, "Thank you."

As directed, he walked down the side of the house and knocked on the door.

A high voice said, "Come in!"

Rob opened the door and went in. He entered a room furnished with a large, wooden desk. Deer and elk heads were mounted on the walls. Filing cabinets, office equipment, and two chairs made up the rest of the office furniture.

The man behind the desk got to his feet. Rob felt disappointed. From the large ranch and ranch house, he had expected John Mackey to be a much bigger man.

Mackey was not even tall. He was several inches shorter than Rob's own six feet. His shoulders were narrow and sloping. A soft-looking potbelly strained against his fancy, tooled leather belt. He was wearing Western clothes, but not the working kind.

His yellow shirt was embroidered and had fringes on the shoulders. His brown pants had a stripe down the sides. His boots were too pointed, and the leather had fancy designs in different colors.

Many men like him could be seen in Arizona, but not usually on a working ranch.

Mackey's eyes were cold and gray as a foggy day. They had a flat, dead look. Rob had seen eyes like that before. They were the eyes of a man who got whatever he wanted—no matter what he had to do to get it.

"Well? Who are you?" Mackey said impatiently.

"I'm Bobby Tyrell, Mr. Mackey."

"Oh, yeah, the parolee. Been expecting you." Mackey gave him a spare smile. He came around the desk and offered his hand. His hand was slightly moist, and his handshake was limp.

Mackey said, "I've hired ex-cons before. I'm always willing to give a man a second chance. But you'll get no favors here. I expect you to work hard and do what you're told."

"I'll do that, Mr. Mackey," Rob said.

Mackey said, "Then you'll do just fine."

The other door to the office opened, and a young woman entered. She was tall and slender with bright blue eyes and blonde hair. She was quite pretty. She looked to be in her late twenties.

She said, "I'm sorry, Daddy. I didn't know you were busy."

Mackey was frowning at her. "What is it, Elaine?" The woman was staring at Rob with frank curiosity. Mackey said again, "Elaine?"

She looked back at him. "It's nothing important, Daddy. I'll come back later." She went out of the room, closing the door.

Rob was thinking that the woman named Elaine didn't look much like her father.

Mackey opened the door and stepped outside. He yelled, "Dan! Come here, boy. I need you."

A few moments later the young man who had told Rob where to find Mackey came up to them. "Yes, Mr. Mackey?"

Mackey gestured toward Rob. He said shortly, "Bobby Tyrell, Dan Acuna. Bobby will be working here awhile, if he pans out. Take him over to the bunkhouse and get him settled in."

He jerked a thumb toward Rob. Obviously, the interview was over.

Rob nodded to Mackey. Without another word Mackey went back into his office and closed the door.

Dan held out his hand. "Glad to meet you, Bobby. Welcome to Shadow Ranch."

They shook hands and started walking.

Rob nodded his head toward the closed office door. "Not the most friendly guy I've ever met."

Dan laughed. "You could say that, yes."

"Is he a good rancher?" Rob asked.

"Not so you'd notice. Of course I don't see the books. But it'd be my guess that he's losing money regularly." They had reached the corner of the house. Dan pointed to a long, low building about a hundred yards away. "That's the bunkhouse. Let's walk over now. You can collect your pickup later and park it over there."

As they walked, Rob said, "If he's losing money, how's he stay in business? Is he a rich man and the ranch a sort of hobby?"

"Not all that rich, I'd say. As to how he stays in business . . ." Dan's face got a secretive look. "I've never quite figured it out. There are some strange things that go on around here."

"Such as?" Rob asked.

Dan shook his head. "It's better you don't ask."

Rob was tempted to ask anyway. But it was too early in the game to arouse suspicions by being too nosy.

Dan said, "If anybody keeps the ranch operating, it's Bert Willis, the foreman. You'll meet him later. Be careful around him. He's a hard nose, but he knows ranching. Just obey his orders and don't ask too many questions. You'll get along okay."

They walked in silence for a moment. Rob glanced at Dan and said, "You're a Native American, aren't you?"

Dan's face closed up. His eyes clouded with distrust. "That make a difference to you?"

"Oh, no!" Rob said hastily. "I'm half Navajo myself on my mother's side."

Dan relaxed. "Welcome, bro." He laughed. "Yeah, I'm Hopi, as is my uncle Will, who works here with me. You know, the Hopis and the Navajos are traditional enemies. But I have the feeling we're going to get along just fine."

"Are you a . . ." Rob paused. "Are you an ex-con too?"

Dan shook his head. "No, my uncle and I are just wandering cowboys. What were you in prison for, Bobby?"

Rob gave Dan his cover story. "I . . . well, I was involved in a drug deal. I went down for pushing. At least that's what the police claimed. Actually, I was in the wrong place at the wrong time. I know, I know!" He held up his hands. "Every ex-con swears he's innocent. I *was* innocent but also stupid. I was drunk and keeping bad company."

"I believe you, Bobby," Dan said quietly. "But Uncle Will says I always believe what people tell me. And I doubt anybody else around here will believe you."

Rob shrugged. "I can live with that. I guess Mr. Mackey hires a lot of parolees?"

"Oh, yeah," Dan said. "Many of the hands are parolees. Some are Mexican. They all work cheap."

"How about you and your uncle?" Rob asked. "You said you weren't ex-cons, yet you're working here."

"But we're Indian," Dan said with a harsh laugh. "We're expected to work cheap. And we needed a job. We'll be moving on as soon as we have a few bucks saved. We have family up on Third Mesa."

They arrived at the bunkhouse and went in. Since it was the middle of the afternoon, the long room was empty. It held about twenty bunks, ten lower and ten upper. There was a large bathroom with showers at one end. The other end held a small recreation area. That section held a number of chairs, two tables, and a TV set on a shelf on the wall.

Rob looked around and caught Dan grinning at him. Dan said, "Doesn't look like much, does it?"

Rob shrugged. "I've seen worse."

"Well, yeah, so have I." Dan laughed. "At least the roof doesn't leak."

"Which bunk should I take?"

"You can pretty much have your pick. Only ten men working here now, so ten bunks are available."

"Well, I guess I'll drive my pickup over—"

He broke off as a body filled the doorway. The man who came in was big, bulky, and approaching fifty. His face was seamed and leathery from long exposure to the fierce Arizona sun. He had a large, hawk-like nose over a tight, unsmiling mouth. His eyes were the color of mud.

The newcomer scowled at Rob. "You the new man?"

Dan said quickly, "This is Bobby Tyrell, Mr. Willis. Bobby, this is our foreman, Bert Willis."

Willis never took his eyes off Rob. "I understand you went down on a drug bust, Tyrell?"

"Yes, but I was—"

Willis held up a big hand. "Don't want to hear if you were innocent or guilty. I don't care. But I stand for no drug use on Shadow Ranch. I catch you at it, you're out of here, and your parole officer is notified. Which means you go back to serve out your sentence."

Rob said quickly, "I don't use drugs, Mr. Willis."

"Glad to hear it." He paused, his hard gaze pinning Rob. "You know why I don't mind hiring ex-cons?"

"No, sir."

"Because they're used to taking orders without talking back. That's what you'll do here, understand?"

Rob said, "I understand."

"Good." Willis started to turn away, then turned back again. "You do your work and keep your nose clean, there may be a chance to earn a few extra bucks now and then." Then he was gone, his big body filling the doorway as he went through it.

Rob said, "What was that all about?"

Dan refused to meet his eyes. He mumbled, "I don't know, Bobby."

"But what did he mean, a chance to earn a few extra bucks?" Rob asked.

Dan shook his head. He still did not look at Rob. "I

don't know, like I said. Sometimes Willis can be . . . well, a little strange."

Rob had a strong feeling that Dan was lying. Why, he didn't know. But again he decided not to push it. He said with a little laugh, "Well, I can always use extra money. I'm not going to get rich with the wages I'm being paid here."

"Bobby . . ." Dan finally looked at him, frowning. "Be careful. Don't get involved."

Rob said, "Careful? What are you talking about, Dan?"

"That's all I can say," Dan said. "I have to get back to work now."

He turned on his heel and left the bunkhouse quickly. Rob stared after him thoughtfully.

Suddenly, Rob felt the hair on the back of his neck rise. He felt a strong feeling of danger. He felt as if he were being watched. He looked around the bunkhouse. Sun came in the west windows, flooding the long room with light. There was no place for anyone to hide.

He laughed at himself. He was jumping at shadows. At Shadow Ranch. He stepped to the door. He could see Dan walking toward the oak tree and the other men. They were finished eating now and were cleaning up, ready to return to work.

Rob liked Dan, but at this stage of the investigation he could not trust anyone.

CHAPTER
2

It had all begun in the State House in Phoenix. Rob had gone to the small office of Stanley Morgan. Morgan was the director of the Governor's Task Force on Crime. The task force had been in existence a little over a year. Rob had joined the group two weeks ago.

Morgan was a short man of fifty with graying hair and steely gray eyes. His features were blunt with a snub nose that gave him a boyish look. He had a slim file open before him. He looked up from it. "Welcome to the task force, Mr. Harding. Do you fully understand our purpose?"

"I think so, sir," Rob said. "The task force was set up by the governor. It was created to investigate certain crimes. Mainly crimes that are hard for other agencies to handle."

Morgan nodded. "That is pretty much it. Tell me, Rob, why did you take the job with us?"

"Well . . ." Rob paused. He was not quite sure how to

answer. "I served eight years in the Army. The last four I was with the Military Police. So when I got out, I looked around for something similar. I liked my work with the MPs."

"Why didn't you re-enlist in the Army?" Morgan asked.

"I just thought it was time to get into something else. I didn't want to make a career out of it," Rob answered.

Morgan nodded. "I read your Army record. It's a good one. Glad to have you with us."

He looked down at the papers on his desk. "You are about to receive your first assignment, Rob. A lot of Native-American artifacts have been turning up on the market. We suspect that a new Indian cliff dwelling has been discovered."

Rob said, "I haven't read anything about any such discovery."

"That's because the discovery was probably made by the person who has been plundering the site. We suspect that someone has stumbled across the cliff dwelling and is looting it."

"And I'm supposed to discover who that is?" Rob asked.

"Yes. You'll be going undercover as Bobby Tyrell. We made up false papers for you." Morgan pushed several papers across his desk. "You have just served two years of a four-year sentence for pushing dope. You've just been released on parole. There is a man named John Mackey. He owns a ranch up in the area I'm talking about. He hires parolees because he can get them for low wages. It's possible that he is involved in these artifact thefts. Your supposed parole officer has already arranged for a job for you on the ranch."

Rob picked up the papers and examined them. Everything was made out in the name of Bobby Tyrell.

He glanced up with a frown. "Why send me on a job like this? I know nothing at all about Native-American artifacts."

Morgan said, "Neither does any other member of the task force. But you have a couple of things in your favor. Some of the people you'll come across up there are Native Americans. Also Mackey hires a lot of Hispanics. According to your resumé you're half Navajo and you speak Spanish fluently. Isn't that right?"

Rob nodded. "Right on both counts."

"Many of the ranch hands on the Mackey ranch are Chicanos and two are Hopi. Any of them may be involved in the thefts," Morgan said.

Rob was silent. He was uneasy about the assignment. He didn't feel he was right for it. But what could he do? This was his first assignment. It would put him in a very poor light if he complained.

Morgan seemed to sense Rob's concerns. He said, "Personally, Rob, I think you're exactly right for the job. All I ask is that you do your best. You do that and everything will be fine. Not to blow my own horn, but I'm very loyal to the men under me. You'll learn that for yourself. Do your best, don't foul up, and I'll stand behind you all the way."

That had been two weeks ago.

Now Rob lay in his bunk, hands behind his head. He was too wound up to sleep. It was after ten o'clock. The bunkhouse was dark except for a dim night-light at the end of the big room. All around him men were sleeping. The only sounds were occasional snores. They sounded like the rasp of dull saws cutting into green wood.

He remembered Morgan's warning. Was John Mackey involved in the theft of the artifacts? From Mackey's cold manner and dead eyes, Rob could well believe that. It struck him that Willis, the ranch foreman, might also be involved.

Rob felt a strange unease here. On the surface Shadow Ranch appeared perfectly normal. It appeared to be a working ranch and nothing more. Yet Rob felt that things were not what they seemed. He drifted off to sleep with disturbed thoughts spinning in his mind.

It was still dark when he was awakened. He heard a cowbell noisily clanging just outside the bunkhouse. A glance at his wristwatch told him that it was six o'clock. Last night Dan Acuna had warned him that they were awakened early in the morning.

Around Rob, others were stirring and talking. A few cursed at being aroused so early.

Rob got out of bed and began dressing. He joined a line in the bathroom at one of the sinks, waiting to wash his face and hands.

A chuckle sounded behind him. "Don't say I didn't warn you, Bobby."

Rob glanced around into Dan Acuna's smiling face. Rob said, "I'm used to it. In prison they roust you out pretty early."

"Was it hard, serving time in prison?" Dan asked. He added quickly, "Maybe I shouldn't be asking. Other parolees here take offense if you ask about prison."

"I don't mind," Rob said soberly. "It wasn't all that hard. For me being locked up was the worst part. But I had it coming. I did a stupid thing."

Dan said quickly, "You don't have to talk about it if you don't want." He shuddered. "I was in jail once—ten days for being drunk and disorderly. It was pure hell, man."

"Like I said, I don't mind talking about it," Rob said. "I got drunk too and was in bad company. It was my first offense. I got a four-year sentence. I served two years and was paroled two weeks ago."

The man in line in front of Rob finished and moved off. Rob took his place at the basin and stopped talking while he washed up.

A few minutes later he walked into the cook shack with Dan. The building was divided into two rooms. The kitchen took up a third of the building. The rest was the dining room. There were two long tables with benches where the ranch hands sat to eat.

The food was good and ample. Platters of fried eggs, ham, and bacon were passed around. A platter of toast was set on each table with pots of butter and jam. Pitchers of orange juice were available and plenty of coffee.

Dan sat next to Rob. The older man Rob had seen yesterday sat on the other side of Dan. Dan said, "Bobby, meet my uncle, Will Acuna. Uncle Will, this is Bobby Tyrell."

Will Acuna held out his hand. Rob shook it. The hand was hard with calluses. With a grave face, Will said, "Pleased to meet you, Bobby."

"Same here," Rob replied.

They began to eat. Rob said, "I must say they serve good food and plenty of it."

Dan laughed. "Oh, they feed you well. I guess they figure that well-fed hands are more likely to give a good day's work."

"I've never worked on a ranch before," Rob said. "What exactly does a ranch hand do?"

"Almost everything. It's hard work," Dan replied. "It depends on the season. You play nursemaid to cows and their calves. You help birth the calves. You pull the cows out of mud. Cows are stupid, you know. You mend fences. You break horses to riding. You even do some farming. Here, like on most ranches, they raise hay. Then you have to dry it. You bale it so they can feed the cattle in the winter when the grass is dead."

Rob shook his head. "I see that I have a lot to learn. I wonder what job they'll start me off with?"

Dan laughed. Even Will, usually grave of face, cracked a smile.

Rob glanced from one to the other. "What's so funny?"

"I think I'll let you find that out for yourself," Dan said.

They had finished eating now and were on their last cup of coffee. Some of the men were getting up and leaving. Bert Willis, the foreman, ate with the men. He sat at the end of the table nearest the entrance. Now each man, as he left the room, paused by Willis's chair. Each one talked to the foreman before walking on.

Dan got to his feet. "You're about to find out your job for the day, Bobby," he said with a grin. "Willis hands out the assignments as we go out."

Rob joined Dan and his uncle as they walked toward the head of the table.

Willis nodded to them. "Dan, you and Will work that fence today in the north pasture. Some cattle broke it down yesterday." His cold gaze came to rest on Rob. "As for you, Tyrell, we go by the seniority system around here. The dirtiest jobs fall to the newest man. Today, you'll muck out the horse barn. When you're done with that, sweep and clean out the bunkhouse." He chuckled. "We don't hire maids on Shadow Ranch."

Scut work, Rob thought. Well, he'd gone through that in the Army. New Army recruits were always handed the worst jobs.

Aloud, he said, "Yes, Mr. Willis. I think I can handle all that okay."

"Just see to it that the bunkhouse is clean by the time the men get back from work," Willis said with a nod. Dan winked at Rob. Rob smiled and walked out of the dining room.

*   *   *

It was going to be a hot day. The horse barn was already uncomfortable. Rob found a shovel and a broom. Four of the stalls were occupied by horses. He knew they must be riding horses, not working horses. He opened the stalls. Then he let the animals out into the fenced pasture behind the barn.

He began cleaning out the stalls. After an hour of heavy labor, he was sweating heavily. He removed his shirt and continued.

Shortly before noon he heard the sound of hoofbeats. In a moment Elaine Mackey rode into the barn on a big bay. The horse was lathered. It had been ridden hard. Rob leaned on the shovel and watched as she dismounted.

Elaine smiled. "You're the new hand, right?"

Rob nodded. "Yes, ma'am," he said. "Bobby Tyrell."

"Hope you'll like it here, Bobby." She handed him the reins. "Would you unsaddle him and rub him down?"

He took the reins. "Yes, ma'am."

She was trim and slender in her riding clothes. He watched her as she walked out. Elaine Mackey was a beautiful woman.

He got busy again. At noon he walked over to the cookhouse and got a couple of sandwiches from the cook.

It was the middle of the afternoon before he had finished with the horse barn. He crossed over to the bunkhouse. He found a broom, a mop, and a bucket and started cleaning.

Between each row of bunks were lockers fastened to the wall. The lockers had locks on them. Rob swept the area between two bunks. As he did, his broom slipped in his grip and thumped against the bottom locker. The locker door flew open. Evidently the owner had forgotten to lock it securely.

Rob bent down to close it and snap the lock. Then he froze. The locker had two deep shelves. On the upper shelf was a pot. Rob glanced around quickly. The bunkhouse was still empty.

He reached in and took out the pot. It was clearly ancient and had crude figures drawn on it. Morgan had given him a book on Indian artifacts. Rob had read it from cover to cover before coming up here.

Rob studied the pot for a few moments. There was no doubt in his mind: the pot was of Indian origin. Was this piece of pottery stolen from the Indian ruins?

He returned the pot to the locker and closed the door. In the door was a slot, and in the slot was a piece of paper with a name. The name was Dan Acuna.

CHAPTER 3

The next morning Rob was again assigned to cleaning the horse barn and the bunkhouse.

As Rob went about his work, his thoughts were on Dan Acuna and his uncle. They had seemed no different this morning. Will was as quiet as ever. Dan was as cheerful and talkative as ever. They had again been assigned fence-mending chores. Could they be involved in looting the cliff dwelling? Rob didn't want to think so. Yet there was the pot he had discovered. Of course Dan could have found it somewhere else. He could have bought it. Maybe it was a gift for somebody. Yet Rob had learned that coincidences seldom happened.

"Good morning, Bobby," said a throaty voice behind him.

With a start Rob whirled around. Elaine Mackey stood in the doorway, smiling at him.

"Good morning, Miss Mackey," he mumbled.

She laughed. "Elaine, please. We're not formal on Shadow Ranch. Could I ask a favor of you, Bobby? Do you ride?"

"I have ridden quite a bit, yes," he replied.

Elaine said, "I'm not riding this morning. Would you take my horse out? He needs the exercise."

"I'd be happy to, Miss . . . uh, Elaine," he said. "But Mr. Willis ordered me to clean the barn and the bunkhouse. He might not be pleased if he finds out I'm—"

"Don't worry about him," she interrupted. "Bert Willis may be the foreman of Shadow Ranch, but Daddy owns it."

"Okay, whatever you say," he said.

While Elaine watched, he saddled the horse. Then he led him outside and mounted up. Elaine perched on the top rail of the fence and watched as he rode off. After a short distance he urged the horse into a trot. Then he drove it into a full gallop. He made a complete circle of the fenced pasture. When it was completed, he reined in before Elaine on the rail.

She said, "You ride well, Bobby."

"I've never really worked on a ranch before," he said. "But I learned to ride when I was a kid."

"I'm surprised you're working here at the low wages Daddy pays," she said. "It seems to me you should be able to earn more."

Rob shrugged. "If you're a paroled convict, you take what you can get."

"Well, maybe something can be done about that." She jumped down from the fence. "Work him out for another half hour or so. And thanks, Bobby."

She walked off, leaving him staring after her. What had she meant by her remark about money? He gave a shrug and reined the horse around for another gallop. It felt good to be riding again.

*   *   *

That afternoon he went in to clean the bunkhouse. The first thing he did was check Dan Acuna's locker. It was firmly locked. He wondered if Dan realized that he had left the locker unlocked the day before.

At supper that night, Rob watched Dan closely. Dan showed nothing. He was as open and friendly as always. After supper, most of the ranch hands went into the bunkhouse to watch TV. Dan and Rob sat at the picnic table up by the main house and talked. The main house was lit up. Rob could hear piano music coming from it.

He said, "Who's playing the piano? Mr. Mackey doesn't strike me as a musician."

Dan snorted. "Nah, not that one. I imagine it's Miss Elaine. She plays. I've heard her before."

Rob asked, "Is she friendly with the hands?"

Dan glanced over at him. "Not that I've noticed. Why do you ask?"

"She spoke to me yesterday. She asked me to rub her horse down after she rode him. Today she asked me to exercise him."

Dan laughed. "I wouldn't call that friendly, man. She wanted something from you, didn't she?"

"Yeah. Does she ride much?"

"Quite a bit. Those riding horses in the horse barn are all hers. Her old man hardly ever rides. He sits around on his duff all day. When he does leave the house, it's usually to drive off in that Cadillac of his."

"Does Elaine get along well with Willis?" Rob asked.

Dan gave a shrug. "Well enough, I guess. Nobody really

gets along well with Willis. Why do you ask?"

Rob said, "She said something today that made me wonder."

"What's that?"

"She wondered why I was working for the low wages her father pays. She said maybe something could be done about that," Rob said. "What do you suppose she meant by that?"

Dan frowned at him. "I don't know, man. But I'd advise you not to mess around with her. Could get you fired. Maybe even get your head cracked open."

Rob said, "It was nothing like that, just idle talk."

He broke off, his glance on the bunkhouse. Bert Willis was leaving the bunkhouse with four men. Rob watched curiously as the five men got into the foreman's pickup. The pickup drove off toward the main road a mile distant.

"Now where do you suppose they're going?" Rob asked.

"Maybe into town for some rooting and tooting," Dan answered.

"Awful late for that," Rob said. "And with the foreman along? I don't think so."

"Maybe you don't want to know where they're going." Dan got to his feet abruptly. He seemed angry. "You know something, Bobby? You ask too many questions. You know what curiosity did to the cat?"

Rob laughed uncertainly. "I'm not a cat, Dan."

"Maybe you'd be better off if you were. That way you'd have more than one life to risk."

Dan walked off with angry strides. Rob stared after him. Well, that had been an interesting reaction. Had it been caused by Rob's remarks about the trip to town? It would seem so.

He got to his feet and stared after the foreman's pickup. It was certainly a mystery. Why would Willis and four ranch hands drive off close to nine o'clock at night? It was an hour's drive to the nearest small town, Camp Verde. By the time they got there, it would be time to turn around and drive back.

Rob shook his head. No, that couldn't be the answer. It had to be something else. Could it have anything to do with the looting of the cliff dwelling?

When Rob entered the bunkhouse, he found that Dan was already in his bunk asleep. Or he was pretending to be. The remaining hands were watching a cop show on TV. Even the ones who didn't speak English were watching.

Rob sat down with them for a bit. But the show was stale and unexciting. Rob finally got up and prepared for bed. He was still not used to the hard labor he had been doing. He was tired. Even with the TV blaring he went to sleep at once.

He was awakened some time later by hushed voices. He didn't know what time it was, but he sensed that it was late. The voices of the men as they prepared for bed seemed strained. Rob was still half asleep. He didn't think about it for very long. In a moment he was sound asleep again.

The sense of tension was still there the next morning. As Rob walked to the cookhouse with Dan, he asked, "All the men seem quiet this morning. Did something happen last night?"

Dan didn't look at him. "I was told that one of the guys who went off with Willis last night disappeared."

"Disappeared?" Rob asked. "What does that mean?"

Dan shrugged. "It means what it means. It was José, one of the Mexican illegals. He just walked off. It's nothing out of the ordinary, man." Dan still seemed angry. "They come up here from Mexico, work for a spell, then just leave. Maybe they get homesick. Maybe they get an idea the

Immigration people are after them. Whatever the reason, they go."

Rob said, "Did you ever learn where they all went last night?"

"They went jacklighting."

Rob looked at him sidelong. "Hunting jackrabbits with spotlights?"

Dan nodded. "That's what I was told."

Just before they entered the cookhouse, Rob said, "Something about this doesn't add up. The guys who were with Willis last night . . . well, they strike me as being scared."

Dan stopped to look at him. "Scared? Man, what is it with you? You've got some imagination! What would they have to be scared about?" He laughed scornfully. "All those big, scary jackrabbits?"

Dan quickened his step and walked on by himself.

In the horse barn a half hour later, Rob noticed that Elaine's horse was gone. While he worked he kept an ear cocked for her return. She was later than usual. He had eaten his lunch and was on his way back to work when he heard loud voices in the barn. He began to hurry.

Inside the barn he saw Elaine by her horse near the stall. A big man stood before her, his back to Rob. Rob moved up quietly behind him.

The man's voice was loud and abusive. "I take my orders from Bert Willis, not you."

Elaine said quietly, "I just want you to unsaddle my horse and rub him down."

"I don't do barn chores," the man said.

Elaine's eyes darkened. "You know who I am. My father owns this ranch!"

The man laughed crudely. "Oh, I know who you are, right enough. You're a good-looking woman is what you are." He took a step toward her. "Tell you what, boss lady. You give me a kiss, and maybe I'll take care of your horse for you."

Elaine's eyes widened. She took a step back. "You touch me and you're fired!"

"Maybe it'd be worth it—"

Rob was directly behind the man now. He clapped a hand on the man's shoulder. He spun him around. He vaguely recognized the man as one of the ranch hands.

The man glared at him out of mean, little eyes. "What are you doing butting in here, bud?"

Rob said steadily, "I think you'd better just walk away, friend."

The man snarled, "I'm no friend to an ex-con. Take your hand off me!"

He swung a ham-like fist at Rob's head. Rob saw it coming. He ducked aside. The fist whistled past his head. Smoothly Rob stepped in. He brought a knee up into the man's groin. The man howled in pain. He doubled up, grabbing at his groin. Rob locked both hands together and brought them down like a club across the man's neck. The man fell to the ground.

Elaine looked at Rob with wide eyes. She said softly, "You handle yourself pretty well, Bobby."

Rob shrugged. "A man learns how to protect himself in prison, or he pays a heavy price."

"I'm used to men like him." She glared down at the man on the ground in contempt. Then she looked up again at Rob. "I've learned to take care of myself. But I'm grateful to you just the same. Thank you."

Rob nodded. The man groaned. Rob leaned down and seized him by the shoulder. He lifted him off the ground. He began to shove him toward the barn door. At the door he gave him a hard push. The man stumbled away for a few steps. Then he caught himself and glared back at Rob.

Rob said tightly, "You'd better move off, friend. And I'd advise you to stay out of Miss Mackey's way from now on."

The man didn't move. Rob took a threatening step toward him. The ranch hand started toward the bunkhouse in a stumbling run. Rob smiled and turned back into the barn.

Elaine hadn't moved. He took the reins from her. "I'll take care of your horse, Elaine."

Elaine said, "You won't regret this, Bobby."

Rob watched until she had walked out of the barn. Then he got busy with unsaddling and rubbing down the horse.

For the rest of the day he kept an eye out for the man who had bothered Elaine. He might try a sneak attack to get even. But he didn't appear. At supper time Rob looked around the cookhouse for the man. He didn't see him anywhere. Probably he'd been fired because of what happened with Elaine, Rob thought.

After supper the foreman was standing by the cookhouse entrance. As Rob started past him, Willis caught his arm. He said, "Want a word with you, Bobby. Outside."

Outside the cookhouse Willis waited until all the other men had walked off. He lit and smoked a cigarette. When the last man was out of hearing, he looked at Rob keenly.

He said, "Miss Mackey told me what happened this afternoon."

Rob was uncomfortable. "Glad I was able to help her. Probably nothing would have happened anyway."

"Oh, it might have," Willis said. "The idiot had been

drinking. He should have been out on the range working. But he told me this morning that he wasn't feeling well. He just wanted to stay here and get blasted."

"I thought he might have been drinking," Rob said.

Willis ground out his cigarette under his boot. "Well, you thought right. And the guy is long gone." He tilted his head. "Elaine tells me that you handle yourself pretty well."

Rob looked away. "I had to learn."

"I can imagine," Willis said in a dry voice. "The thing is, this whole bit has cost me another hand. And I guess you heard that a man walked away last night."

"I heard," Rob said with a nod.

"Could you use some extra money?"

Rob said, "Who couldn't?"

"There's a little project going that has nothing to do with the ranch," Willis said. "I need someone to replace the guy who left. You interested?"

Rob felt a quick thrill. Was it going to be that easy? Was he being hired to help loot the cliff dwelling? Of course, it could be something else entirely.

He managed to keep his face expressionless. "It depends."

Willis gave a nod. "On the money, of course. It'll be worth your while. Of that you can be sure. Probably triple what Mackey pays you."

"Then I'm interested."

"It's not strictly on the up-and-up. At least not according to some people. I don't happen to agree with them. There's no violence involved, no real crime, in my opinion."

Rob said, "Then you can count me in." He laughed shortly. "So long as it doesn't violate my parole. I don't want to go back to prison."

"I won't lie to you, Tyrell. There is a slight risk of that, but very slight."

Rob paused for a few moments. He wanted Willis to think that he was weighing the risk, however slight. And he didn't want to appear too eager. He shook his head. "I don't know, man. I sure don't want to go back. On the other hand, I sure could use some money." Finally, he nodded. "I'm in."

"Good!" Willis clapped him on the shoulder. "It's all night work. Meet me at my pickup in an hour. We'll work most of the night. But don't worry. I see to it that the men who work with me on this have the next day easy. You leave that up to me."

Rob said, "Okay, Mr. Willis."

Willis said, "Welcome aboard, Tyrell." With a nod he walked off toward the bunkhouse.

Rob watched him go. He still hadn't learned what it was he would be doing. But he thought he could guess. So far, so good. It was all going smoothly. The thought made him nervous. He had learned early in life that anything good seldom came this easily. But this was what he was here for. It was his job. If there was some risk, so be it. He was paid to take risks.

CHAPTER 4

Three of the workers who left the ranch in Willis' pickup were Hispanic. The fourth, a man named Jake Thomas, rode in the cab with Willis. Rob rode in the back with the other three. He soon learned that none of the three spoke much English. He didn't let them know right away that he spoke Spanish well. He thought he might learn more if he kept his mouth shut for a while.

They had to share the bed of the pickup with picks, shovels, sledgehammers, and baskets. There were also several Coleman lanterns and an ice chest. The night was very dark. There was no moon. They drove to the main road and headed north. After a few miles Willis turned off onto a dirt road. It was a good thing the pickup had four-wheel drive. The road was little more than two ruts in the ground. They were heading east now.

It was a very rough ride. They were bounced around in the truck bed. Once the vehicle hit a deep pothole. If

28

Rob hadn't been holding on to the side of the bed, he could easily have been thrown out.

The only light came from the powerful headlights of the pickup. Rob tried to make a mental map of where they were traveling. He might need it later. It was very difficult.

He knew that the Mogollon Rim towered some seven thousand feet to his left. He judged that they were heading slightly northeast now. That was the direction of the Rim. Yet it was so dark that he couldn't see the mountains. He would have a hard time following their path later by himself.

Now he realized that they were beginning to climb slightly. The Hispanics in the pickup bed with him had said little since they left the ranch. Now they began talking among themselves in low voices. Rob could only catch a word or two. He could sense fear and tension in their voices.

What were they afraid of? Were they all in danger of some kind? Maybe he would soon find out.

He twisted around to look ahead. He saw that they were entering a canyon. In the pickup's bright headlights he could see walls rising steeply on each side.

One of the men with him spoke. "Secco Canyon!" He sounded fearful and excited at the same time.

After about two miles, the climb became steeper. The pickup's motor was working hard. They were moving at only a few miles an hour now. The road twisted and turned like the trail of a snake.

At last they came to a stop. The driver's door opened. Bert Willis said, "We're here. Everybody out."

Rob got down with the other men. He looked around. He could still see very little. Willis gave the order to unload the tools from the pickup. Then the men shouldered the tools. Rob followed their example.

Willis said, "This way, men." He started on a narrow trail up the side of the mountain. He carried one of the Coleman lanterns that lighted their way.

They hiked up the mountain for several minutes. There was no sound except for the sound of the men's boots on the trail. The trail was steep. Rob felt the weight of the heavy pick and shovel he was carrying. Then the man ahead of him stopped. Rob raised his head. The light from Willis' lantern showed a wall of stone in front of them. The men put down their tools and sat down to rest.

Willis and two of the other men lit the rest of the lanterns. Then two men picked up a ladder well hidden behind low shrubs. They leaned it against the wall. The top of the ladder disappeared into the darkness above.

One of the men began to climb the ladder. He was wearing a hat with a flashlight on the brim. It was easy to follow his progress. Up and up he went. He looked like a spider against the light-colored stone.

Above the man there was a large, dark shadow. As the man drew closer Rob could see what it was. It was the mouth of a large cave. He had been right. This could only be a cliff dwelling. Willis had to be after artifacts.

When the man reached the cave mouth, he climbed onto the ledge. Then he began dropping down ropes so the tools could be hauled up.

In a short time Rob found himself standing on the ledge. In front there was a long drop to the trail. Behind him was what looked like a small city built into the hollow of the rock. The houses, or rooms, were packed together wall to wall. Rooms were stacked on rooms. The open windows and doors looked like empty eyes.

Someone whispered, *"Ciudad del muerto."* City of the Dead. Rob shivered. He felt it too. They had no right to be here.

Willis' loud voice broke the spell. "All right, men. We haven't finished in the big room yet. So let's get back to work. Remember, pick up anything that you find. Pots, statues, baskets. And be careful. These things are worth more money if they're in one piece."

Rob watched to see what the other men did. They were picking up lanterns, baskets, and tools. He did the same. Then he followed them through a dark doorway.

Inside, lantern light cut through the darkness. He felt a great awe. He was standing in a large room with a low ceiling. In the center was a shallow pit blackened by fire. Smoke from its many fires had blackened the walls and ceiling. This must have been a meeting place. What had they been like, those ancient people?

Rob shivered. He felt a thrill of fear. Could the spirits of a long-ago people still linger here? Was that what caused the fear he had sensed in the others? Willis motioned the others forward. They crossed the room and entered another chamber. This room was somewhat larger. Here there were signs of digging. Mounds of dirt stood everywhere. Holes and trenches gaped in the ground like wounds. The room smelled musty.

The lanterns were set so they lighted the floor. Willis held Rob back out of earshot of the others. Willis said, "I don't figure you for a stupid man, Tyrell. I guess you know what's going on here."

Rob nodded. "Yeah. You're looting Indian artifacts and peddling them."

"Right," the foreman said. "Any objections?"

"None that I can think of."

Willis nodded again. "Good. Some guys get pretty uptight about it. The way I figure it, these things belong to whoever finds them. The fact that there's a good market for artifacts means big bucks for all of us."

"Like I said, I can use the extra money," Rob said.

Willis said, "I didn't want to tell you what all this was about before. I didn't want you running to the authorities. Now that you're involved you can't run to them. You do, you'll land in hot water along with the rest of us."

"Don't worry," Rob said. "I'll keep my mouth shut. Looks to me like this is the golden goose. I don't want to kill it."

Willis grinned. "Smart thinking, Tyrell. Now pick up a shovel and get to work. This room has been a gold mine. Evidently it was a storeroom. We've already picked up most of the stuff that was above ground. There were a lot of big jars and baskets. But there is still stuff underneath from even earlier times."

Rob got a shovel and moved over to where the other men were working. Two pits had been dug. Neither was more than three or four feet deep.

Rob stood for a moment in indecision. Willis came over. He motioned to an untouched area a few feet off to the right. The foreman said, "Why don't you start a new trench, Tyrell?"

Rob stepped to the area indicated. He took a pick lying nearby. He began digging carefully.

He felt very nervous. This work should be done by professionals. Yet he was here. He had to make it look as if he were only interested in the money to be made. To act any other way would raise suspicion. Also he realized that he would have to continue. He couldn't just stop with this one night. He now knew that Willis was in charge of this crew. But there had to be somebody else behind it. He was sure that the man behind the scene was Mackey, the ranch owner. That was the person that Morgan was after. Arresting Willis would not uncover the leader.

Rob began to dig. He had to wonder why the foreman had placed him apart from the other men. Was Willis afraid? Did he think that the men might say something that Willis didn't want Rob to know?

His shovel struck a hard object. Rob knelt by the hole he had dug. Again he ignored the foreman's instructions. Rob did not try to pry the object out with the shovel. He carefully dug it out of the earth by hand. He lifted it to the light. It was a small cooking pot. It was blackened by many fires. There was a feeling of great age about it. How long had it been since living people had fed themselves with food cooked in this pot? Rob placed the artifact carefully aside and continued digging. An hour passed. Rob didn't unearth another artifact in that time.

Willis clapped his hands for attention. "Okay, guys. Time for a break." In Spanish he said, "Manuel, you and Pedro go to the truck and bring back the ice chest."

The two men scrambled to their feet. One said, "*Si, Señor!*" Manuel and Pedro quickly left the chamber.

Willis picked up one of the lanterns. "I'm going to prowl around some of the other chambers. I want to see which one offers the best opportunity. I think we've about mined all we're going to in this one. Give me a yell when those two get back."

Jake Thomas said, "Okay, boss."

Willis went through the low doorway into the next chamber. Jake sat down against a wall and fired up a cigarette. Rob sat down beside him.

Jake grinned at him. "Hard work, huh?"

"I've done worse," Rob said. "I'm curious. How was this place found?"

Jake blew smoke. "Way I get it, Willis stumbled onto it one day while he was out hunting."

"Odd that it was never found before. After all, it's been here a long time."

Jake laughed. "You got that right, Tyrell. A long time. The thing is, it's pretty well hidden up here. Willis told me he was tracking a cougar when he found it. Few people ever come into Secco Canyon. No reason to. When we leave every night, we brush out the tracks. The chance of anyone ever stumbling onto it is pretty small."

Rob had many questions he wanted to ask Jake. But the two Hispanics returned just then with the ice chest. Willis was called. Perhaps just as well, Rob thought. If he asked too many questions now, Jake might get suspicious.

The ice chest contained sandwiches, a gallon Thermos of coffee, and a six-pack of beer. The others all took a beer. Rob settled for a paper cup of coffee.

Jake asked, "You don't drink, Tyrell?"

"Booze is what got me into trouble in the first place," Rob replied.

A half hour later they were at work again. Rob worked steadily. The size of his excavation grew. He found two more pots and four objects that looked like crude tools. By his watch it was three o'clock in the morning when Willis called it quits.

The foreman said, "We have to get out of here and back to the ranch before daylight. Load up and let's hit the road."

The artifacts were carefully packed away in paper

boxes and stored in the pickup. They all piled in. Willis headed the pickup back down the mountain.

Rob noticed the men in the truck with him. They were looking back fearfully at the cliff dwelling. He heard one of them speak rapidly in Spanish. The man muttered the name José several times.

Rob decided now was the time. In Spanish he said, "Excuse me. You're speaking of José, the man who worked with you before me?"

The man gave him a startled look. "*Si*, Señor. José Mendes."

"The man who just walked away?"

The man shook his head vigorously. "No, Señor. He did not walk away. He fell."

Rob blinked. "Fell? I don't understand."

"*Si*, fell." The man pointed up toward the cliff dwelling. "From up there."

"How did that happen?" Rob asked.

"When we left the rooms we saw—" The man drew a fearful breath. "We heard a flute playing. Then in the doorway to the room we saw a figure. The figure was very tall. It had a round head. On top of the head was something, a topknot, feathers. I couldn't see. The body looked like that of a dead man. Like a skeleton."

One of the other men shuddered. He whispered, "It was Masau!"

Rob said, "Masau?"

"*Si*. The Skeleton Man. Masau, a god of the Hopi!"

Rob looked slowly from face to face. "Then what happened?"

Manuel said, "He started toward us, playing his flute. We started to run. But José, he—"

"Yes?" Rob prompted.

"He ran the wrong way. Mr. Willis tried to stop him. But José ran around him. He fell—fell to his death!"

Rob said, "How do you know he's dead?"

"We found him. We buried him and said the prayer for the dead over his grave."

Rob was shocked. "The police weren't told?"

Manuel shook his head. "Señor Willis, he said it was not wise. We have no green cards, Señor. The Immigration people, they would arrest us. They would send us back to Mexico."

Rob fell silent. He stared straight ahead. He was absolutely stunned by what he had just learned.

CHAPTER
5

Rob faced a problem. He
thought about the dead man buried in Secco Canyon. It
disturbed him. The death should be reported to the police.
On the other hand, if the police were brought in now, it
would break the whole case wide open. Rob's identity
would be uncovered. Willis would be arrested, but the
person behind the looting would forever remain a secret.

Rob finally decided to leave the decision up to Morgan.
He should call him anyway. He hadn't been in touch since
he'd been given the assignment in Phoenix. Today was
Saturday. He would have Sunday off. He could drive into
the nearest town, Camp Verde, and make the phone call.

There was one decided benefit in working with Willis
and the looters. Rob no longer had to clean the horse barn
and the bunkhouse. He was promoted to helping mend
fences. Rob had to smile to himself. He wasn't sure if
"promoted" was really the right word. But it was certainly
better than doing scut work.

He was teamed with the Acunas on the fence mending. Rob realized that both men knew that he hadn't been in his bunk until very late last night. Yet they said nothing. Maybe they knew nothing about the looting of the Indian ruins. Rob found that hard to believe. Yet, it was possible. Maybe only those ranch hands directly involved knew of the ranch foreman's nighttime activity.

Both Acunas were quiet as they worked. Rob was used to that from Will, but Dan was usually talkative.

The summer sun was hot. All three had their shirts off by mid-morning. Most of the work consisted of stringing new wire to replace the old. It was really hard work. The worst thing about it was the barbs on the wire. All three men were wearing heavy gloves. Even with the gloves, Rob's fingers soon became bloody and ripped.

Rob tried to get a conversation going with Dan. "How does all this wire get broken?"

"Mostly because the cattle push against it," Dan said curtly. "Sometimes they get spooked by something. Then they stampede right against the fence, snapping the wire right off."

Dan fell silent. Clearly Dan wasn't in the mood for talk. Rob wanted to ask the men if they knew about the looting. But if they didn't, it would be a mistake.

Finally Rob asked, "You guys are Hopis, Dan. What do you know about Masau, called the Skeleton Man by some?"

Both men stopped working and stared at him. With a scowl Dan said, "Where did you learn about Masau?"

"Oh, I overheard some of the hands talking," Rob said with a shrug. "The guys said that Masau was one of the Hopi gods."

Will Acuna grunted. "They have no business speaking of Hopi matters. They know nothing."

"Masau is the Hopi god of the underworld, among other things." Dan said quietly. "He is chief god of the Hopi."

Rob looked from one to the other. From the expressions on their faces he knew he was pushing it. Still, he needed to know. "Have you ever heard of this god appearing in person to non-Hopis?"

"Appearing?" Dan frowned. "Appearing where?"

Rob gave a shrug. "Oh, just around. Some of the men said they had seen him."

Dan shook his head. His expression was hard. "You know what I said to you before, Bobby? What is it with you? You're too nosy!"

Rob backed a step. "Don't get your shorts in a twist, Dan. I don't know much about the Hopi people." He laughed. "Or very much about the Navajos, for that matter."

Dan took a step forward. "Then learn it somewhere else!"

Will Acuna placed a hand on his nephew's shoulder. "Leave it, Nephew. Just leave it."

Dan resisted for a minute. Then he shrugged and turned away. The two men moved off and began working at a distance from Rob. They remained that way for the rest of the afternoon.

Rob was puzzled by Dan's reaction. But he also kept away from them. It wouldn't be wise to push it any further right now. They stopped work early and headed back to the ranch.

Rob went into the bunkhouse and took a long shower. His mind buzzed with questions, but he had nobody he dared ask. It was best just to let it be for now. In the morning he would make the call to Stanley Morgan.

After his shower he changed into fresh clothes and walked outside. The sun was still up. But Shadow Rock now cast its shadow over the ranch buildings. The temperature had dropped by at least ten degrees. It was pleasant in the shadows.

None of the other ranch hands were in sight. Rob felt at loose ends. Maybe he should go back in the bunkhouse and read. Or he could watch TV. Neither activity appealed to him.

He strolled toward the horse barn. It smelled not unpleasantly of horse droppings and old saddle leather. All the stalls were empty except for the one holding Elaine's bay horse. Through the open door he could see the other horses grazing in the meadow.

He walked to the stall. The horse snorted, rolling its eyes. Then it moved to the stall door and stuck its head over the door.

Rob laughed. "Good horse," he murmured. "Where's your mistress?" He scrubbed the animal's neck with his knuckles.

A voice behind him caused Rob to jump. "I'm right here, Bobby."

He whirled around to see Elaine coming toward him. "Miss . . . uh, Elaine."

She stopped before him. "I missed you this morning when I took my ride."

Rob laughed. "I've graduated. Mr. Willis took me off scut work and put me to mending fences."

She raised an eyebrow. "Scut work?"

"It's an Army term. The raw recruits always get the bottom-level jobs. Washing dishes, peeling potatoes, cleaning latrines. Things like that."

"Didn't take you long to graduate, did it?" she said with a smile.

Rob warmed to her smile. "Just lucky, I guess."

"I told Bert that you were worthy of a better job. For once he listened to me, I guess."

"Thank you," he said.

She studied him for a few moments in silence. "You said you like to ride. Tomorrow's Sunday. Maybe you'd like to ride with me." She laughed lightly. "The hands say they do enough riding during the week. They don't care to do it on their days off."

Rob hesitated. "I'm sorry, Elaine. I'd like to very much. But I have to drive into Camp Verde tomorrow. I have some errands to do."

Again she was silent. As she looked at him her eyes were soft and warm. Then she nodded abruptly. "Perhaps another time then."

"I'd like that very much."

With a nod she turned on her heel and walked away.

Rob absently rubbed the horse's neck. He watched Elaine until she was out of sight. Was she flirting with him? Why would the owner's daughter come on to a lowly ranch hand, an ex-convict? It made no sense.

Yet Rob found it flattering. Maybe if he wasn't involved in the investigation he could show more interest.

At supper, Rob didn't know if the Acunas would want to sit with him. It had become a habit. But after the way they had reacted to his questions today, he wasn't sure. As he started past where they sat, Dan gave him a smile. He patted the bench beside him. "Come on, Bobby. Sit."

Rob sat down. "I wasn't sure."

Will Acuna said, "We Hopi are a little touchy when asked questions about our religion. There has been so much publicity about it. People read about our Snake Dance, for instance, and think we're weird."

"I meant no disrespect," Rob said quickly.

Dan placed a hand on his arm. "I realize that, Bobby. I apologize. I reacted too quickly."

"It's no big deal, Dan," Rob said. "I can see why you acted the way you did. Forget it."

They began to eat. Dan didn't say anything for a few minutes. Then he spoke, "I'd still like to know who told you about Masau. And why."

"It was one of the Hispanics. Manuel, I think his name is," Rob replied. "As to why, I have no idea." He wanted to tell them what he'd heard about the man who had died. He decided that would not be a good idea.

They ate for a little in silence.

Then Dan set his fork down. "So the hands have been seeing Masau, have they? That's very interesting. I wonder if they were someplace that they had no business being?"

Will gripped his shoulder. "Let it drop, Nephew. It's nothing for us to concern ourselves with."

Dan subsided. He flashed a sidelong glance at Rob. "Uncle's right, Bobby. Let's all just forget it. Hey, what do you think of the Cardinals' chances this year?"

Rob was a little startled. It was the first time either of the Acunas had shown any interest in football. He said guardedly, "Not very much. They need some new offensive linemen. In fact, they need just about everything, in my opinion."

*   *   *

Rob left the ranch before noon the next morning. He thought of asking the Acunas to go into town with him. But they had disappeared somewhere. He didn't know any of the other hands well enough to want them along.

Stanley Morgan had given Rob his home telephone

number. Even though it was Sunday, he could be contacted. He had told Rob back in Phoenix, "I want you to call me any time, day or night, if there's a problem. Any member of the task force working undercover can always get in touch with me. You're out there alone enough as it is."

Camp Verde was a small town. Either Cottonwood or Sedona was much larger. Rob had never liked large towns. Camp Verde had a little flavor of the Old West to it. He liked that. Rob thought he might drive to Cottonwood later and take in a movie. But first he stopped at a service station to make his phone call and fill the gas tank on the pickup. There was a pay phone on the station wall. He would much rather have called from a booth. But public phone booths were out of fashion nowadays. He would just have to keep an eye out. He did not want anyone to overhear him. The phone was answered on the third ring. A child's giggle sounded in Rob's ear.

He said, "Could I speak to Mr. Morgan, please?"

The giggle sounded again. "Daddy's in the backyard."

"Would you get him, please? Tell him it's Rob Harding calling."

The phone was banged down hard. Rob winced as his eardrum vibrated. At least the kid hadn't hung up. A couple of minutes passed. Rob wondered if the child had told Morgan there was a call for him. Rob had little experience with children. An only child himself, Rob had lived a lonely childhood.

A voice said in his ear, "Rob? Is that you?"

Rob came back to the present with a start. "Yes, Mr. Morgan. I wasn't sure that—"

"Sure that Shelly would fetch me?" Morgan chuckled. "Oh, she isn't very good on the phone, but she always rounds me up. After all, she's only five."

Rob didn't quite know how to respond to that.

He was silent for a moment. Morgan said, "I assume you're calling to report in. Have you found out anything?"

"I think I have," Rob replied.

"Then suppose you get on with it," Morgan said.

Rob related what had happened so far.

Morgan said, "Sounds to me like you're doing fine. After all, it's been less than a week. You've learned that there *is* a cliff dwelling being looted. You've learned that people at Shadow Ranch *are* involved in the looting. But I gather that you think there's someone higher up in charge?"

"Yes, sir," Rob said. "I'm convinced of it."

"Then forge ahead, Rob. You've justified my faith in you." Morgan paused for a moment. "But I have the feeling you've something more to add."

Rob said, "Yes, sir, I have. A man died up there two nights ago."

"How? Was he murdered?"

"I don't think so," Rob said. "It seems to have been an accident." He related what Manuel had told him.

Morgan said, "Masau? A Hopi god? It's getting a little weird, isn't it?"

"You might say that." Rob hesitated. "I thought of calling the police, but I knew that would probably blow my cover. I thought I'd call you first."

Morgan was silent for a few moments. "You did the right thing, Rob. If it was murder, it should be reported. But since it isn't, we'll wait. Our primary concern here is nabbing whoever is behind the looting. Keep this man's death under your hat for a bit. If any heat comes down later, I'll take the blame. But hurry things along as much as you can, Rob."

"I'll do my best, Mr. Morgan."

"I'm sure you will. If you get a chance, call me back in the middle of the week. Let me know what's coming down."

"I will, sir."

"And, Rob," Morgan hesitated again, "if this death is by any chance murder . . . well, you be careful. Your life could be in danger. It's a remote chance, but it's possible."

"I'll be careful," Rob promised.

He hung up the phone. He stood for a few moments in deep thought.

A voice behind him said, "Tyrell? Bobby Tyrell?"

Startled, Rob spun around. Jake Thomas stood smiling at him. He was wearing a short-sleeved shirt and casual pants. His graying hair was slicked back. His brown eyes had a puzzled look.

"I thought that was your pickup parked over there," Jake continued. "Who you calling?" He grinned. "Not to be nosy."

Rob had recovered his wits. "Oh, that. My parole officer. I'm supposed to call him once a week."

Jake frowned. "Parole officer? On a Sunday morning? You mean you called him at home?"

"Yeah. He's down in Phoenix," Rob said. "I'm supposed to report to him once a week. Driving all the way down there and back on a work day would be a drag. So he was nice enough to tell me I could cover it with a phone call on the weekend."

Jake laughed. "Never heard a parole officer called nice before. That's a first." He studied Rob carefully. "Want to have a drink with me? I know it's early, but what the hey."

"I'm sorry, Jake. I'd like to, but I have some errands to run. It's going to take me the rest of the day. Maybe another time."

Jake's brown eyes narrowed in suspicion. Finally he shrugged. "Okay, Bobby. See you back at the ranch."

Rob watched Jake as he walked away. He got into a dusty, ancient car. Before driving away, he sat for a few moments staring at Rob. Finally he started the old car and drove off.

Rob was filled with anxiety. Had Jake Thomas trailed him here from Shadow Ranch? Some investigator he was if Jake had followed him and he had not seen him!

The other explanation was that it was a coincidence. But Rob had never believed in coincidences. Had Jake believed the story about calling his parole officer? Would he report back to Bert Willis?

One thing was certain. Rob knew that he was going to have to be doubly careful from now on. Morgan could be right. He could be in grave danger.

CHAPTER 6

Rob looked down at the plate of sausage and eggs in front of him. He did not feel very hungry this morning. He had spent a restless night and was feeling tense. Had he aroused Jake Thomas' suspicions yesterday? Had Jake said anything to Willis?

Rob went to Willis to get his work schedule. Willis seemed very friendly. His face wore what might have been a smile.

"Miss Mackey has told me you're a good rider, Tyrell. Also, I understand that you speak Spanish?"

Rob wondered where this was going. He nodded. "Yes."

"We've got a problem. Some cattle have drifted away from the main herd up on the mesa," Willis said. "They've drifted down into one of the draws. The grazing isn't very good there. They could stay in the draw until they starve to death. Take one of the Mexicans. Ride up there and drive them back to the main herd. It'll probably take most of the day."

Willis looked around. They were alone in the cookhouse now. "But that's okay. We won't be working tonight. Here. This is how many cattle are missing."

He gave Rob a slip of paper. Rob took it and left the cookhouse. He felt much relieved. Apparently his cover was still safe.

The man Rob chose to help move the cattle was Manuel. This was the man who had told Rob about seeing Masau. Rob thought he might learn more from him.

He found Manuel and told him in Spanish that they would be working together. Manuel nodded. His expression was wary. He did not look very happy.

Rob didn't push things. They went to the stables and chose their horses. Rob chose a trim bay mare that he had noticed earlier. She wasn't as fine a horse as Miss Mackey's mount, but she had good lines.

Manuel chose the big roan. The two men began to saddle their mounts. By the time they were finished, things were easier between them.

It was a two-hour ride out to the small canyon where the cattle had strayed. It was rough country and hard riding. Rob found little chance to talk to Manuel.

It was noon before they found the cattle. Rob was relieved to see that the animals were bunched together. He counted them. Great! They had stayed together.

He smiled at Manuel. "We've been lucky. They're all here. We won't have to hunt for strays. Let's eat lunch."

Manuel smiled at the mention of food. The ranch cook was noted for his great packed lunches.

Rob pointed to a large oak tree and dismounted

under its shade. They hobbled the horses nearby to graze. Rob unloaded the saddlebags. They held sandwiches, fruit, and some cans of soda. Manuel began to eat hungrily. Rob leaned back against the tree and looked around. Gathering up stray cattle was much easier work than mending fences. Rob felt that he could come to like ranch work.

But first there was his job to do.

He finished chewing a bite of sandwich. "Manuel, do you have a large family?"

"*Si*, Señor. A wife and five little ones." Manuel took a swallow of soda. "It is hard in Mexico. There is no work, but there are mouths to feed."

It was a story Rob had heard many, many times before. The Mexicans had little choice but to cross the border in search of work. It was illegal, of course. If they were caught, they were sent back. The workers would wait for a little while and then sneak across again. It was the way of life.

"I know," Rob said. "And I can't say I blame you, Manuel. How long have you worked at Shadow Ranch?"

"I have been here over a year, Señor Tyrell."

"Bobby. Please, Manuel, call me Bobby." Rob hesitated. "And how long have you been helping with the work in the cliff dwelling?"

"Three months." He looked at Rob almost pleadingly. "The pay is very good. My family back home needs the money badly."

Rob said, "But you do know it is illegal? Against the law?"

"*Si*, I know that." Manuel looked at Rob again. This time it was a sly look. "But you are doing it too."

Rob had to laugh. "You're right, I am. But it's different with me. I'm already a convicted criminal. You're not, are you, Manuel?"

Manuel wagged his head from side to side. "No."

Rob said, "If you're caught, you would go to jail. And you have your family to think about."

"I have thought long and hard about that. But the money," Manuel said. "My Maria and the children need the extra money. The money is worth it."

They both fell silent, eating. So far, Manuel had not seemed put off by the questions. Rob decided to push it a little. "Willis is in charge of the dig. Right?"

Manuel nodded. He looked puzzled.

Rob went on. "Is there anyone else? I mean, is he the top boss? Or is there someone over him?"

Manuel frowned. "I do not understand."

"Is Bert Willis taking orders from someone else? Or is he all on his own?"

Manuel slowly shook his head. "I do not know of anyone else. Señor Willis is the boss."

Rob hid his disappointment. He asked, "This Masau, the Hopi god—have you seen him more than once?"

"No, but one of the other workers said that he did."

Rob said, "How did that happen?"

"He went outside the dwelling to relieve himself," Manuel said. "He saw the Skeleton Man dancing in the moonlight on top of the cliff. He was very frightened and ran back inside. He told only me what he saw."

Manuel was becoming visibly upset. Rob figured that he had asked enough questions for now.

Rob got to his feet. "Time to get back to work, Manuel."

They mounted their horses and began rounding up the stray cattle. The animals were calm. An hour later they herded them all out of the box canyon. It took them another hour to move them to the main herd.

It was late afternoon by the time they arrived back at the ranch. It would soon be time for supper. Both Rob and Manuel showered and got into fresh clothing.

An hour after supper Rob was sitting alone at the picnic table. He was enjoying the quiet and the evening's coolness. He saw Willis and Jake Thomas emerge from the bunkhouse. They headed for the foreman's pickup. On impulse Rob got into his own pickup. He waited until the foreman's pickup drove away. Then he fell in behind them. He didn't turn his headlights on. He stayed well back so that he could barely see the other pickup's taillights ahead.

When they reached the highway Willis turned his pickup in the direction of Camp Verde. Rob stopped his pickup at the highway. He watched Willis' taillights disappear into the night. It seemed certain that Willis wasn't driving to Secco Canyon. Rob sat for a few minutes in deep thought.

Then he put the pickup in gear and drove onto the highway. But he drove north instead of south. He was following his mental map. He hoped that he remembered correctly. Soon he came to the dirt road where Willis had turned east that night when they had gone to the canyon.

Rob knew that he was taking some risk driving to the cliff dwelling. But he would have to explore the place alone sooner or later. Now seemed as good a time as any. Willis and Jake Thomas seemed safely out of the way.

At last he found Secco Canyon. He drove into it to where the trail began. He was pleased that his memory had not failed him. He parked the pickup in the same place where Willis had parked the other night. He took out the flashlight he had bought yesterday in Camp Verde.

He stood for a moment before starting up the path. There was a full moon, but the sky was cloudy. The night was very quiet. Then he heard the yip of a coyote in the canyon. It was followed by another. Then it became a chorus.

Lightning forked the sky to the southeast. Thunder rolled like distant drums. The air smelled of moisture. The summer rains would soon be moving in.

Rob switched on the flashlight. He followed its beam up the trail leading to the cliff dwelling. Finally he reached the rock face. He took the ladder from its hiding place. He leaned it against the cliff. He felt a shiver race down his spine. He was sure there was no one here. Still, there was a feel of danger about the cliff dwelling.

Rob smiled to himself. He had never thought of himself as superstitious. However, there was something about this place. It stirred the hairs on the back of his neck. He started to climb.

He reached the ledge without difficulty. The ruins looked even eerier now that he was alone. He took a deep breath and entered the ruins.

He didn't know what he expected to see. There were only the piles of dirt and holes in the ground. It was cool in the room. He had left the warmth and humidity outside.

He crossed into the next chamber. This was the one where he had worked with the others when he was here. The only difference here was that the dirt was fresher. And someone had left behind a shovel.

He went into the next chamber. It would seem that the cliff dwelling was a series of interlocking rooms. The only outside entrance that he had seen was the one in the first room.

Rob found eight chambers. At least that was the number he could get into. Some of the walls had crumbled. Under the debris there might well be entrances to other rooms.

In several of the rooms there were no signs of excavation. Rob was sure that Willis would loot all the rooms before he was through. That would give Rob time to dig out the identity of the person in charge.

Suddenly Rob had a thought. He leaned against a wall in the next to last room. He shined the light beam around the walls. Whoever was really in charge of the looting must come here to check on what was going on.

All I need is a battery-operated video camera, Rob thought. The camera could be hidden in a hole dug into a wall. Aimed at a doorway, it would record everyone who entered the ruins. At the very least, it would tape Bert Willis overseeing the looting. That would provide strong evidence in court. The ideal place would be in the first chamber. That one was no longer being worked. That meant there was less chance of the camera being discovered.

Rob didn't have such a camera, of course. He would have to contact Stanley Morgan again. The camera could be sent to him in Camp Verde by General Delivery.

Rob was pleased by this idea. It could mean the solution to the problem. With a lighter step he entered the last chamber. The room was very large. There was a round pit in the center. Rob examined it more closely. It was quite deep and at least twenty feet around. The walls were sheer. It looked like the pit had been chiseled out of the rock.

Evidently there had once been a cover over the pit. Rob could see debris littering the bottom. There were long poles. Some of the poles were broken. But there were enough poles to have formed a top, or a cover, for the pit. And to one side of where Rob stood were the remains of a ladder. The ladder had also been made out of poles.

What could have been the purpose of the pit?

He recalled reading that the Hopi used such covered pits as ceremonial centers. They were called kivas. He also remembered something else. The Hopi used snakes in their religious rites. He shivered. He had always been a little afraid of snakes. He flashed the light down into the bottom of the pit. To his relief he saw no snakes.

The pit had no bearing on his case that he could see. But his interest in the people who had once lived here was growing daily. He knew little about his Native-American heritage. When he was finished with this case, he was going to read all he could find on the subject.

He heard a noise behind him and started to turn. He was given a mighty shove in the back. The flashlight flew out of his hand. He fell headlong into the pit. He was lucky that the bottom of the pit was filled with soft dirt. Even so, he was stunned.

For the next few minutes everything was a blur. Finally he gave his head a shake and sat up. The room and the pit were as black as the darkest night. He couldn't even see his hand before his face.

He strained his ears. He heard nothing but the sound of his own breathing. He called out, "Hello! Is there anybody up there?"

There was no answer. He felt foolish. Someone had crept up behind him and pushed him into the pit. That someone had meant him harm. They would hardly come to his rescue now.

Who could it have been? Had someone followed him from Shadow Ranch? Or had someone been waiting here for him? Had Willis tricked him? Had he only pretended to drive toward Camp Verde?

Rob shook his head again. It did little good to worry about who had pushed him. All that could wait until later. Right now he had to concentrate on finding a way out of the pit.

He closed his eyes and tried to see the pit in his mind's eye. The sides were sheer, straight up and down. He couldn't remember seeing any kind of handholds. The pile of dirt he had landed on wasn't even close to being high enough to help him.

He had to try. He got to his feet. He strained his eyes. He could see nothing. Since he didn't smoke, he didn't even carry matches. He stepped forward. He caught himself listening for the deadly sound of rattles. He let his breath go, as he heard nothing. He held his hands out before him until he struck the wall. He reached up as far as he could. There was nothing to grab hold of to lift himself.

He made his way all around the pit until he was sure there was no way out. He fought back a wave of panic. He could yell for help until he was hoarse. No one would hear him.

Of course he wasn't in all that much danger. Eventually, Willis and the looting crew would be back at work. Rob knew that he would hear them. All he would have to do was yell. They would come and get him out.

But that would undo all his work. There was no explanation that he could give to explain his presence here. Willis would assume that he had come here to steal some of the artifacts on his own. Or he would know that Rob was snooping. Either way, he would be fired.

Rob went tense. Had he heard a sound? He listened. There, he heard it again! The scrape of a footstep.

He shouted, "Help! I'm down here! In the pit!"

There was no response. Rob listened intently. He heard another footstep, then another. Had the person who pushed him into the pit returned? Rob choked back the urge to call out again.

Then something whistled through the air. It struck the side of the pit near where he stood. Rob reached blindly out. His hand hit something long and slippery. He drew back. His first thought was that a snake had fallen into the pit.

But it was still there, swinging back and forth. Rob reached out gingerly. His fingers closed around . . .

A rope! It was a rope. Without further hesitation he clamped both hands around the dangling rope. He went hand over hand up the rope. He used his feet against the wall to guide him. After a few moments he felt a current of air against his face. He realized that he was at the top.

He heaved himself out and sprawled on the ground. His feet were still dangling over the edge. He felt the rope go slack in his hands. Then he heard running footsteps. His rescuer was running away.

Rob shouted, "Wait! Don't go! I want to thank you. Who are you?"

There was no answer. It was just as dark up here as it had been down in the pit. He hadn't gotten even a glimpse of his rescuer.

Was it the same person who had pushed him into the pit? Had the idea been just to frighten him?

He pulled his legs out of the pit and stood up. He faced the pit. He tried to remember in which direction the flashlight had fallen. He had been holding it in his right hand. He got down onto his hands and knees. He swept his right hand over the ground slowly.

He was about to give up when his hand struck something. He closed his hand over the object. It was the flashlight. He found the switch and pressed it. Light bloomed in the chamber.

He got to his feet. He faced about and flashed the light around the chamber. It was empty. He aimed the beam of light at the ground. The ground here was hard-packed. It showed no footprints.

He moved slowly toward the entrance. A few feet before he reached it he saw a pile of loose dirt. He fell to his knees. There in the dirt was a footprint! He put his face down inches from the print. It seemed to be the print of a moccasin.

He sat back on his heels. Had the person who had rescued him been a Native American? Or did someone just want him to think so?

Rob shook his head, puzzled. This case was becoming stranger and stranger.

CHAPTER 7

Rob slept badly that night. He had crept into the bunkhouse around midnight. As far as he could tell, none of the other hands had noticed him come in. He undressed quietly and got onto his bunk.

He had thought that he wouldn't be able to sleep. But he fell asleep at once.

He began to dream. The dream quickly turned into a nightmare. He was in a deep pit. He was trying to climb out. But the skeleton man would not let him. The figure danced, laughing at him. A bony foot shot out. Rob was struck in the face and tumbled down into the pit again.

Over and over again he clawed his way out of the pit. Each time he was sent falling back. His fingers flowed blood. His nails were broken. His muscles ached to the very bone.

He awoke with a strangled scream. For a moment he didn't know where he was. Then he realized that he was in his bunk. Daylight crept into the bunkhouse like dirty dishwater. He glanced quickly around. Apparently his scream hadn't awakened anyone.

Rob was soaked in sweat. He felt as tired as if he really had been in that pit again. He didn't go back to sleep. He lay quietly until the cowbell clanged outside the bunkhouse.

He got up and got dressed with the others. While he was headed for the cookhouse, he saw the Acunas.

He nodded. "Good morning, Dan, Will," he said.

Dan smiled with good cheer. "Morning, Bobby. Sleep well?"

"Like a log," Rob lied.

Will Acuna merely nodded. Then he gave Rob a long look. It seemed to Rob that the look held some deep meaning. But he couldn't figure out what that was. Just outside the cookhouse they met Jake Thomas

Thomas said curtly, "Morning, Tyrell."

"Morning, Jake," Rob said in turn.

Rob's thoughts were troubled. Had it been Jake Thomas who had pushed him into the pit? It was clear that Jake didn't like him. It was also clear that Jake was suspicious of him. But if Jake had pushed him into the pit, he wouldn't have rescued him.

Bert Willis was already seated in the cookhouse when Rob entered. He looked up at Rob and nodded without speaking. He gave no indication that there was anything on his mind but his breakfast. Jake was already seated on the foreman's right. He looked at Rob without expression.

Rob passed on down the table to take his seat beside Dan Acuna. Rob was relieved that neither Jake nor the foreman showed any reaction. But he was deeply puzzled. Who had attacked him in the cliff chamber? If not Jake or

Willis, then who? He thought about it while he ate. He reached no conclusion.

Outside, heavy, black clouds were moving in from the south. The summer storms usually came late in the afternoon. Yet, just as Rob finished eating, lightning flashed brightly outside. A clap of thunder shook the cookhouse. Rain hit hard.

Bert Willis got up and stepped to the door to look outside. After a few moments he came back. He didn't resume his seat. He spoke loudly, "Doesn't look like we'll be doing much outside today. But lightning and thunder like this can spook the cattle. Jake, you'll ride with me. Choose a couple of the best riders to go with us. Take those used to herding cattle in the rain. The rest of you work in the horse barn. You can mend the saddles and such. Whatever needs doing."

Jake stood and pointed out the men he wanted to go with them. Rob and the Acunas were left behind with a few other men.

As the men left the cookhouse, Willis lingered. He motioned to Rob and stepped over to the corner of the room. Rob joined him.

"We'll not be going to the cliff tonight, Tyrell," Willis said in a low voice. "There's danger of flash floods in weather like this. It happens several times a year in Secco Canyon. This doesn't make me happy. We're falling behind. But there's no help for it. I have no wish to be caught in a flash flood. We'll have to work harder and longer. Maybe tomorrow night."

Willis turned on his heel and left the cookhouse without another word.

When Rob stepped out of the cookhouse, the rain hit him hard. The wind was strong. The wind drove the rain into his face. It stung like needles.

Rob made a run for the horse barn. Those men who were to check on the cattle were wearing rain slickers. They gathered up saddles and bridles and went outside to round up their horses.

Rob and the other hands began checking the equipment. Rob worked with the Acunas.

Dan chuckled. "For once I'm happy I'm not a top cowboy. I'd sure rather be in here out of the rain than riding in that storm out there."

Rob had to agree. It was a lazy morning. The repair work was all easy. It also could be done sitting down. About mid-morning Rob noticed that all conversation had stopped. He glanced up. All the men were staring at the entrance of the barn. Elaine Mackey stood just inside. She caught Rob's glance and beckoned.

With reluctance Rob put down the bridle he was working on and started toward her. Someone behind him gave a low, mocking whistle. Rob knew that he was in for some kidding later.

Elaine drew him aside, out of the hearing of the others. She said, "Would you run an errand for me, Bobby?"

"Be happy to, Elaine."

"I have some mail that needs to be sent by Special Delivery," she said. "But I'm also expecting an important phone call. Could you drive into Camp Verde to the post office for me?"

Rob was pleased. He had been wondering how he could come up with an excuse to drive into town. He needed to make a phone call to Stanley Morgan. This would provide the perfect opportunity.

He kept his face expressionless. "Of course I'll be happy to do it, Elaine. But Mr. Willis ordered me to work in here today. If he comes back and finds me gone—"

Elaine gestured inpatiently. "Don't worry about Bert Willis, Bobby. If he asks about you, I'll set him right."

Rob nodded. "Fine then."

"Here's the envelope." She handed him a large, manila envelope. "And thank you, Bobby."

As Rob left the barn, he heard another wolf whistle behind him. He grinned and waved a hand as he went through the door.

A few minutes later he was on his way to Camp Verde in his pickup.

He mailed the envelope first, then made his phone call. As usual he was put through to Morgan immediately.

"Mr. Morgan, this is Rob Harding," he said into the phone.

"Rob! I didn't expect to hear from you so soon," Morgan said. "I hope nothing's wrong?"

"No, nothing's wrong," Rob said. He had already decided not to mention the attack on him. "But I need something. I paid a visit to the cliff dwelling last night. I need a video camera. One that can film in low light. It needs to have a motion sensor. I want to plant it in a chamber of the ruins. I figure that the person behind the looting must keep track of what's going on. I think he must visit the cliff when no one else is around."

"I think you're probably right, Rob," Morgan said. "And you have a good idea there."

Rob said, "Then can you send me a camera? Send it to General Delivery in Camp Verde?"

"I can do better than that," Morgan said. "I happen to know a man on the Sedona police force. About six months ago one of the task force investigators needed that kind of camera. The Sedona police were happy to oblige. I'll call the station there. It'll be waiting for you."

"Then I'd better scoot right over there," Rob said. "I'm on an errand for Elaine Mackey. If I'm gone too long, she may get suspicious."

"Fine, Rob. Good luck." Stanley Morgan hung up.

* * *

After picking up the video camera, Rob sat for a few minutes in the pickup. He was deep in thought. What he was thinking of doing was risky. Yet he needed to plant the camera as soon as possible. It would be almost impossible to hide it at the ranch. The rain had stopped. The clouds had all blown away. The sky was so blue it hurt his eyes to look at it.

He decided to go for it.

He drove back to the intersection of I-17, the main highway. He stopped at a service station and made a purchase. After that he drove on north on I-17. Then he turned off on the dirt road leading to Secco Canyon. There was the chance that a flash flood had hit the canyon. Rob hoped that this had not happened. The rainstorm earlier had appeared to be headed east.

The farther he drove, the more his guess seemed on the mark. The dirt road was muddy, but not all that bad. The ground was soft, so Rob parked on the road. Then he took the camera and a small shovel from his pickup. He hoped no other vehicle would come along while he was gone.

At the cliff dwelling, he found a spot in the wall directly across from the entrance to the first chamber. He took the small shovel and made a hole big enough for the camera.

The camera was state-of-the-art. It contained a sensor that switched it on when it sensed any motion. It turned itself off again when the motion ceased. The batteries, he had been told, were good for at least twenty-four hours of filming.

Rob fitted the camera into the hole. Then he went back outside. In a way, the rain had been an advantage. It had turned dirt along the ledge into mud. He had to make three trips to collect enough mud to pack around the camera. It would dry into the same adobe that lined the walls. It would have a fresher look about it, of course. But he did not think that would matter. The looters were no longer working in the front chamber. The odds were good that the newer adobe would not be noticed.

When he was finished, he left the chamber. When he returned to the pickup, he gave a sigh of relief. There were no signs that any other vehicles had been on the narrow road. He made fresh tire tracks while turning the pickup around. Before driving off, he got out and did the best he could to brush those tracks away. It wouldn't pass close inspection. But Willis only came into the canyon at night. The signs should not be noticed. Rob got into the pickup again and drove away.

*   *   *

Rob glanced at his watch when he parked alongside the bunkhouse. He had been gone over three hours. That was twice the time it should take to mail a package at the Camp Verde post office. He had what he hoped was a good explanation.

He saw Bert Willis striding toward him. The foreman was scowling in displeasure. "Where have you been, Tyrell?"

Rob said, "Miss Mackey asked me to run an errand for her."

"She told me. To the post office in Camp Verde. That's an hour and a half round trip at the most. You've been gone over three hours, Tyrell."

"I ran into a problem. My pickup broke down," Rob said.

Willis laughed shortly. "Yeah, right."

"It happens to be true. My fan belt broke several miles out of town. I had to hike back to a service station and buy a new one. Then hike back to the pickup and install it." Rob took out the receipt for the fan belt. "See?"

Willis took the receipt and studied it. "Show me."

Rob tripped the lever to raise the hood. He pointed to the fan belt. "Look for yourself."

Willis bent down to look at it. Then he straightened up. He gave Rob a glare and stalked away without another word.

Rob laughed softly to himself. He looked at the brand-new fan belt. He had used it to replace a perfectly good one less than two hours ago.

CHAPTER
8

The next day dawned cloudless and warm. Yesterday's rainstorm had left the air heavy and humid.

After breakfast Willis called Rob aside. "Tyrell, I want you to do some riding today. Ride the southeast fence. Check to see if any wire is down."

Rob said, "Yes, sir."

Willis made a small motion for Rob to hold back. As he waited, Rob noticed Will Acuna in the doorway. Will was staring at him. The man's look was odd and it made Rob feel uneasy.

Then the room was empty except for Willis and Rob. The foreman beckoned Rob forward. He spoke in a low voice. "Don't overdo yourself today, Tyrell. If it doesn't rain, we'll be going to the cliff tonight. So knock off early and come back to the ranch. Maybe snatch a few winks. We'll be working our butts off tonight to make up for lost time."

Rob nodded. "Will do, Mr. Willis."

Rob got a lunch bag from the cook. Then he went to the pasture behind the barn. He selected a strong-looking paint horse. He slipped a bridle on him and led the animal back to the barn. He saddled the horse and mounted up. Then he rode south at an easy gait.

It was a pleasant ride. The air was fresh. It smelled of growing things. Rob didn't mind the humidity. It made a change from the usual Arizona dryness.

By noon Rob judged that he had covered roughly ten miles of fence. He had discovered only three breaks. He could fix them himself with a pair of pliers.

After mending the last break, he found a shade tree. He hobbled the horse to graze while he ate his lunch.

The sky was still cloudless as he headed back to the ranch. It seemed that they would work the cliff dwelling tonight. He arrived back at the ranch in mid-afternoon. He unsaddled the horse and turned him loose in the pasture.

In the bunkhouse he took a long shower. Then he lay down across his bunk. He lay on his back, hands behind his head. He stared up at the ceiling in deep thought.

His plan was coming together nicely. The next few days should bring him all the evidence he needed. The only problem he foresaw was checking on the camera. It would be too risky to check while he was working at the ruins. There would be other men working nearby. Getting away from the ranch at any other time would be difficult.

Oh, well, some way would come to him. On that thought he fell asleep.

A soft voice was speaking in his ear, "Bobby? Bobby, wake up."

Rob jerked awake. Elaine Mackey was bending over him. He suddenly remembered that he was wearing only his shorts. He pawed at the top sheet and pulled it over him.

Elaine laughed softly. "Sorry to wake you, Bobby."

Rob felt a tug of alarm. "Is anything wrong?"

She shook her head. "No, no. I never got a chance to thank you for running my errand yesterday."

"It was nothing," he muttered. "Happy to do it."

She was looking at him intently. "Bert told me you had car trouble. At least let me pay you for the fan belt."

He waved her off. "No need. It's not that big a deal."

"Then maybe . . ." Elaine gnawed at her lower lip. "How about if I buy you dinner in payment?"

Rob scooted up on his bunk. He was careful to keep the sheet around him. "There's no need, Elaine. But I think I'd like that."

"It's a date then." She turned her head to listen at the sound of men's voices outside. "Saturday night? Say, seven?"

Rob nodded. "That would be nice."

She was gone then, gliding like a ghost. She was out of the room in seconds. Immediately afterward the men poured into the bunkhouse. They hurried past Rob's bunk toward the showers.

Rob wondered if they had seen Elaine leave the bunkhouse. He didn't think so. No one had ragged him about it.

Rob sat for a while, thinking back over the last few minutes. Why had Elaine invited him to dinner? He felt a throb of excitement over the prospect. Elaine Mackey was an attractive woman. Rob wasn't blind to the fact that he was a handsome man. Was that all there was to it? Mutual attraction? Or did she have an ulterior motive?

A short laugh escaped him. If his plan worked, his investigation might be all over by Saturday night. He would have all he needed to nail her father as the man behind the looting. If that happened, Elaine wouldn't want to have dinner with him. She would never want to speak to him again.

He felt a small twinge of regret.

The first men out of the showers were coming into the room now. They ignored him. They laughed and talked together as they got dressed for supper.

Rob got off the bunk and got dressed himself. When he stepped out of the bunkhouse, he looked up at the sky. A few clouds were moving slowly to the south. Otherwise, it was clear. It didn't look like it would rain tonight. That meant that they would work the cliff dwelling.

* * *

They piled into the foreman's pickup at a quarter to eight. Again, Jake Thomas rode in the cab with Willis. Rob sat in the bed with the others.

Manuel beamed at him. "*Hola*, Bobby! I am glad we are working again. I got a letter from Maria. We are having another *niño*. I will need the extra money."

"Hello, Manuel," Rob said. "And congratulations on becoming a father again."

Rob couldn't help feeling some degree of guilt. If his plan worked, men like Manuel would suffer. At worst, they could be arrested and sent to prison. At best, they would lose the money they were earning. True, what they were doing was against the law. But Rob felt bad about them anyway.

They rode most of the way to Secco Canyon in silence. The rutted road leading to the cliff had dried. The foreman's pickup had no trouble. Soon they arrived at the clearing where Willis parked the pickup. They all got out.

Willis said, "We're going to work hard tonight and longer hours. We have to make up for the time we've lost." He waved a hand. "If you uncover some good stuff tonight, you'll be paid extra."

The Hispanics, especially Manuel, brightened at this bit of news. They stepped up the pace of unloading the pickup bed. Shortly they were at the base of the cliff. It was a dark night. The top of the ladder was hidden by darkness.

Jake Thomas started up the ladder first. The Mexican workers were next. Then Rob went up. As Rob climbed, he glanced to the south. As he did so, a spear of lightning stabbed the sky. He could smell rain. But the storm was far to the south. The odds were that it wouldn't strike here.

The men crowded into the first chamber. Rob could not resist a glance across the room to where the camera was planted. Even with the lanterns lit, the far wall of the chamber was in shadow. There was little danger of the camera being discovered. Rob felt a small thrill at the knowledge they were being filmed. The camera would record Willis' presence in the cliff dwelling. He could never claim that he knew nothing about what went on here.

Now Willis said, "We'll start work in the third room today. The second one has about dried up, I think."

They passed through the second chamber into the third. With a shudder Rob recalled the last chamber and the pit. He would never forget the time he spent down there in the darkness.

They set to work immediately. They worked mainly in silence. Rob was suddenly aware of how isolated they were. Here, in the third chamber, they could hear no sounds from the outside.

The room proved productive. At the end of four hours' work, they had uncovered a dozen objects. Most of them had been scarcely damaged by the passing years.

It was midnight when Willis announced, "Okay, guys. Let's take a food break. You're doing good. Manuel, you and your buddy fetch the ice chest."

The two men obeyed the order happily. Rob leaned back against the wall. He was tired and sweaty. Jake Thomas squatted on his heels nearby. Willis walked over to inspect the pile of artifacts they had collected.

Manuel came running back into the room. With heaving breath he said, "Señor Willis, it is raining! Very hard!"

Willis said, "What?! There wasn't a cloud in sight when we got here."

"It is raining very hard. It has been raining for a time."

Willis cursed loudly. "We'd better get out. I've seen what a quick, hard rain can do in these canyons."

Jake said, "What about what we dug up, Bert?"

"Leave it," Willis said curtly. "We don't have time. We have to move. Now!"

They all hurried out of the chamber. Outside, Rob saw that Manuel was right. Clouds hovered low overhead. Thunder rumbled like cannon fire. The rain slanted down in sheets. A strong wind blew huge raindrops against his skin. They felt as solid as hail.

Willis motioned them toward the ladder. Rob thought they would probably be safer remaining here. The cliff dwelling was quite high. A flash flood would have to fill the canyon halfway up the cliff to reach the dwelling. Yet he sensed that it would be a waste of time to argue with the foreman.

They scrambled down the ladder. The rungs were wet and slippery. Twice Rob slipped and almost fell. Finally he reached the ground. The others were ahead of him, racing for the clearing and the pickup. The ground was muddy and slick. Water was running inches deep.

Willis was already in the truck cab when Rob reached it. The pickup started to move away. Rob flung himself at the pickup bed. He caught onto the gate. Manuel leaned over to help him. Manuel heaved and lifted him into the bed.

Rob nodded his thanks. It was raining even harder. Thunder rumbled constantly. It was impossible to speak. Flashes of lightning made the night as bright as day. Rob was soaked through. The rain was cold. He huddled in the pickup bed shivering.

Manuel leaned over and shook Rob. He had a frightened look. He pointed behind them with a shaking finger. Rob sat up to look. Lightning forked the sky. Rob's breath caught. About a hundred yards behind them rushed a wall of water. It stretched from canyon wall to canyon wall. It was about ten feet high and growing higher.

Rob twisted around and pounded on the cab window. Jake turned. Rob pointed at the wall of onrushing water. Jake caught on immediately. He leaned over to shout in Willis' ear.

Without hesitation Willis wrenched the wheel to the right. The pickup swerved off the road toward the nearest canyon wall. Rob knew that it was the only thing left to do. They could never hope to outrun the water. The canyon wall was about twenty-five yards away. It was a desperate move. Rob knew it was their only hope. If the rolling water struck the pickup, they were finished. Every monsoon season people were drowned in canyon flash floods.

But the pickup didn't make it to the canyon wall. It began to slow. It plowed ahead a few more feet and stopped. The vehicle was bogged down in the mud. Willis raced the motor. It was useless. The wheels spun. The truck sank even deeper.

Rob gripped Manuel's arm and motioned him out of the truck. Even as they clambered out, the cab door flew open.

Willis tumbled out. Jake jumped out of the passenger side. They all headed at a dead run for the canyon wall.

Rob risked a glance back at the roaring water. He could hear it now. It sounded like the roar of a train engine. It seemed to Rob that the water was much higher now. And it was much, much closer.

Could they reach high ground in time? If they didn't, they would be seized like toys scooped up by a giant. They would be tossed and tumbled and pulled down to a cold, watery death.

CHAPTER 9

Rob had not known that he could run so fast. The roar of the water behind him seemed to push him forward. They were running up a slight incline. They were moving toward the base of the canyon wall. They were within a few yards of it now. But how could they climb the wall? There seemed to be no way up.

The wall of onrushing water was dangerously close. Rob fell against the wall. Looking up, he gasped for breath.

Beside him Willis shouted, "How do we get up the blasted thing? We have only a minute or two!"

Then Rob saw it. "There!"

He pointed to his right. A few feet away two ropes came sliding down the canyon wall. They were barely visible in the driving rain. Willis grabbed one and began to climb hand over hand. Jake Thomas pushed past Rob and started up the other rope. Rob motioned to Manuel to follow Willis.

Rob glanced to his left. The wall of rushing water was only a few yards away. In a flash of lightning he saw that the water was reddish with mud. The tumbling crest of the wave was laced with broken branches. He turned to the rope and seized hold.

He began to climb hand over hand. He was afraid that the water would hit before he was out of its reach. If that happened, he would be torn from the rope. He would be sucked down into the raging water. He climbed faster.

The wall of water struck. It hit his legs from the knees down. It sucked at him, pulling. Rob scrambled desperately, lifting his legs out of the way. The water let him go, rushing on.

He glanced up. To his surprise the others had disappeared. In another flash of lightning he saw that the cliff bulged out close to the top. The two ropes disappeared over the bulge. For an instant he thought that he saw something. It looked like a bony figure standing on the very edge of the mesa. The figure gazed down at him. The figure looked just the way the Hopi god, Masau, had been described to him.

Rob blinked and the figure was gone. Had he imagined it? Now Manuel poked his head out a few feet above Rob's head. Manuel stretched a hand down and shouted something. His words were lost in the roar of the rushing water.

Reaching up, Rob took Manuel's hand. Manuel gave a mighty heave. Rob was lifted high. He saw now why the others had disappeared. There was a ten-foot-wide ledge below the bulge in the cliff. All the others were there.

Manuel heaved again. And then Rob was sprawled on the ledge. He struggled for breath. Suddenly he realized that the rain had stopped. He looked up at the dangling ropes disappearing into the darkness above. He looked at Willis.

The foreman shook his head. "We'd never make it up there. Not over that bulge of rock up there. Besides, there's no need to. We'll be safe here until the water goes down."

Jake said, "Who do you suppose is up there?"

Willis shrugged. "I have no idea. It's a mystery to me."

"Whoever it was saved our necks," Rob said.

"There's that," Willis said with a nod.

Manuel said unexpectedly, "It was Masau. I saw him."

Willis stared. "What? You mean that Hopi god you guys have been telling me you've seen?" He gave a snort of laughter. "Don't be ridiculous. There's no such thing. Probably a couple of cowboys who got caught in the storm. They saw us about to get wasted and tossed the ropes down."

Rob started to say that he thought he'd also seen Masau. He changed his mind. He said, "Why didn't they let us know who they are?"

"Who knows?" Willis replied. "Maybe they didn't want anybody to know they're out here. Who cares?" He stared out at the surging water below. "I know one thing. My pickup is gone. If we ever find it, it'll be a piece of scrap."

"Better that than our lives," Rob said absently. "The water seems to be going down."

"Yeah," Willis said. "It's peaked. Daylight should be here soon. The water should be gone by then. We can walk out. May have to slog through mud up to our knees, but we can make it."

Rob said, "Won't we be missed? Won't somebody come looking?"

Willis gave him a sharp glance. "Nobody knows where we are, and it's going to stay that way. Understand, Tyrell?"

"I understand," Rob answered.

"Be sure you do."

Two hours later daylight began to creep over Secco Canyon. The water along the bottom of the canyon no longer ran high and angry. It was reduced to a trickle. The sky was cloudless.

"We might as well get going," Willis said with a sigh.

The foreman was the first man to slide down the canyon wall. Soon they all stood at the bottom of the canyon. Rob took a last look up at the top. No one appeared. Clearly, whoever had rescued them had left long ago.

By the time they reached the road, the mud was ankle deep. They started out of the canyon. A half mile farther along they came across the foreman's pickup. It had lodged against a large boulder well off the road. They walked over to examine it.

The bed had been torn loose. The cab was crushed flat. The motor had been torn from its mountings and lay several yards away. Rob was awed by the destructive power of the flash flood.

Willis cursed. "Ruined. And it's not even paid for."

"Well, it's insured, ain't it, boss?" Jake said.

Willis glared at him. "It's not the same, Jake. Sure, I'll get a new truck with the insurance money. But it's like losing an old friend." He motioned. "All right, let's go.

We have a long walk."

It was indeed a long walk. It was mid-afternoon by the time they reached the ranch house. They were all tired and cranky. Jake Thomas was limping badly. Just before they reached the bunkhouse, John Mackey came boiling out of the main house. He hurried toward them on his short legs. His face was red.

He started talking before he reached them. "Where the devil have you been, Bert?"

The others were too tired to be much interested and headed on toward the bunkhouse. Rob lingered to listen. Willis caught his glance and jerked his head toward the bunkhouse.

Rob heard Willis say, "I'm sorry, Mr. Mackey, but I got caught in a flash flood. My pickup was totaled. Lucky no one was hurt."

Rob heard no more as he entered the bunkhouse. Glancing back, he saw that Willis had the ranch owner by the elbow. He was leading him away toward the main house. Rob would have given anything to have been able to hear all of their conversation.

There was a small window in the recreation area of the bunkhouse. It overlooked the main house. Rob rushed over and peered out. Mackey and the foreman were nearing the house. Just then Elaine came out to meet them. All three seemed to be talking at once as they entered the house. Once again, Rob would have given anything to be a fly on the wall.

He stepped away from the window and headed back to the shower room. His clothes and boots were caked with mud. He would worry about that later. Just now, he wanted only to get his body clean.

Later as he strolled up to the cookhouse for dinner,

Rob noticed Mackey and Willis. They were driving away from the main house in the ranch owner's Cadillac. Rob didn't think they would be going to Secco Canyon, not in the Cadillac.

No one mentioned the fact that six men had been missing from the bunkhouse. No one except the Acunas.

As they began to eat, Dan said, "I noticed that you and Jake and the others didn't sleep in last night. Where were you?"

"We all went jacklighting," Rob said.

"Again?" Dan said with a shake of his head. "That's getting to be a habit. Bert Willis should be getting good at it by this time."

Will Acuna said, "I noticed that the foreman's truck is missing. What happened to it?"

Rob continued with the lie he'd prepared. "He may not be hunting jackrabbits for awhile. We all got caught in a flash flood last night. His pickup was totaled."

"Pretty costly hunting, I'd say," Dan said in a dry voice. "Caught in a canyon, I'd guess?"

"Yep, Secco Canyon," Rob replied. He watched the faces of the two men. He hoped to catch a reaction at the mention of Secco Canyon. But there was no change of expression at all.

The subject was dropped after that. The talk moved on to other subjects, to Rob's disappointment.

Rob had had no sleep at all last night. He was beginning to feel it. He went to bed right after supper. He went to sleep at once. He slept right through until the morning cowbell clanged.

*   *   *

Bert Willis was at his usual place for breakfast. Rob

felt rested after a good night's sleep. He was also very hungry. After breakfast he hung back until all the other hands had received their work assignments. Then he approached the foreman.

Willis leaned back with a sigh. "Morning, Tyrell. Quite a night we had, huh? Look, we're going to have to hold off on the cliff dwelling for a few days. I have to replace my truck. I looked for one in Cottonwood last night. Nothing caught my eye. So I'm going into Phoenix today. Probably stay overnight."

Rob nodded. "I'm sorry you lost your pickup, Mr. Willis."

"Well, I'm past that now," Willis said. "Anyway, you take it easy for a couple of days. You deserve it after what we went through. You ride fence today and tomorrow. You finished with the south fence?"

Rob nodded.

"Okay, take the north fence today. Take your time. Take today and tomorrow on it. Take along a bedroll if you like. Spend the night out under the stars." Willis winked one eye.

Rob said, "Okay, Mr. Tyrell. I may do just that."

Rob was quite happy with the day's assignment. It solved his problem. He could ride to the cliff and check the hidden camera.

In the horse barn he noticed that Elaine's horse was gone. She must have gone riding early this morning. Rob caught one of the horses in the pasture. He threw a saddle on the animal and rode north. Once out of sight of the house, he sent the horse into a gallop.

He didn't ride into the canyon right away. He rode up the slope onto the mesa running along the top of the canyon. At last he came to the spot above the ledge where they had climbed the ropes. He dismounted and cautiously approached the edge. The ropes were gone now. But he knew this was the spot. Two sturdy pines grew a few feet from the edge. There were scuff marks on the trees where the ropes had been tied. Somebody had taken the ropes. Rob searched for footprints. The ground was mostly rock. It showed nothing.

Rob mounted up and turned his horse back. An hour later he was riding down the canyon. His eyes on the ground, he saw fresh hoofprints in the partially dried mud. He was seized with a feeling of excitement.

It was clear that whoever had ridden the horse was headed for the cliff. Rob was very excited. He didn't even consider the possibility that he might be riding into danger. When he rode into the clearing at the foot of the cliff, there was no horse or rider in sight.

Rob dismounted quickly and climbed up the ladder. He burst into the first chamber without any thought of caution. He went directly to where the video camera was hidden. He opened it and took out the tape. Quite a bit of it had been used.

His plan had worked!

Of course, he couldn't be sure until he had seen the videotape. To be on the safe side, he slipped in another tape. Then he returned the camera to its hiding place.

He left the room quickly. He was eager to get into town and find a place to view the videotape.

CHAPTER
10

Rob stared at the TV
screen, stunned. He couldn't believe what he was seeing.
He was in a video shop in Sedona. He had just watched
the tape from the video camera in the cliff dwelling.

He rewound the tape and ran it again. The result was
the same. He sat back, deep in thought. His plan had
worked all right. But he had been wrong about the guilty
party. It was not John Mackey. Or so it seemed.

Rob left the video shop. He pocketed the tape and a
copy he'd made. It was the morning after he had taken
the tape from the cliff dwelling. Bert Willis still had not
returned from his truck-buying trip to Phoenix. After
breakfast this morning Rob had driven into Sedona. He
didn't ask permission. He didn't much care if this caused
some problems. He thought his job here would be over
after he looked at the videotape.

Now he wasn't quite so sure.

The big question was, what to do now?

He spotted a pay telephone at the corner service station. He walked over to it. Let Stanley Morgan make the decision.

But Morgan was not in. His secretary said that he had been called away unexpectedly. It was a family emergency.

Rob was taken aback. "Didn't he leave a number to call?"

"I'm sorry, no. He did say he would call me sometime tomorrow," Morgan's secretary said. "Can I take a message?"

Rob was silent, thinking. Finally he said, "That won't do. There's no way he can get in touch with me. I'll call tomorrow. Ask him to leave a number where I can reach him."

She said, "All right, Mr. Harding."

Rob hung up slowly. He stood for a moment. What should he do now? Act on his own? He remembered one of the first things he had learned in police work: never barge into a dangerous situation without backup. Yet, this wasn't that dangerous a situation. All that was involved was the theft of artifacts. That was serious enough, certainly. But the penalty only amounted to a heavy fine and perhaps a light prison sentence.

He could go to the local police. But what good would that do? He had little proof to back up his story. He didn't even carry papers identifying him as a member of a special task force.

Stanley Morgan had told him why in the beginning. "None of my investigators carry anything but their cover identification. That may cause you difficulty at times, but it's best. I'm always only a phone call away, Rob."

Only this time the supervisor wasn't just a phone call away.

There was one thing he could do. It would provide some insurance. In the shop he'd made a copy of the video. He got into his pickup and drove to the Sedona post office. He addressed the package to Morgan's office and mailed it.

It was late afternoon when he drove up to the ranch. The hands had already knocked off work for the day. They were lounging around, waiting for the supper bell. Dan Acuna and his uncle were sitting at the picnic table. They were watching him.

Rob arrived just in time to see John Mackey driving away in his Cadillac. Without further thought Rob parked in front of the main house. He got out, the videotape in his hand. He went up the steps to the front door and rang the bell.

The door opened. Elaine stared out at him. "Bobby! I looked for you earlier. Where have you been all day?"

"I had something needed doing," he said. "May I come in?"

She hesitated briefly. Then she nodded and stepped back. Rob stepped inside. She closed the door after him.

Rob showed her the videocassette. "There's something I'd like you to see. Do you have a VCR?"

Elaine stared at the cassette for a moment. Then she looked up at him. "Of course, but what is this about, Bobby?"

Rob said, "I think it best you view the tape first."

Elaine motioned for him to follow. They went down the dim hall to a room toward the back. The room had comfortable furniture. There was a large TV set against one wall and a bar. It was clearly a family room. Elaine motioned to the TV. She sat down on the couch facing the set. Her face was wiped clean of any expression. Yet Rob sensed that she was very tense.

He slid the tape into the VCR and turned on the TV. When the TV had warmed up, he punched a button on the remote control. He sat down in an easy chair at an angle to the couch. From there he could watch Elaine closely.

The screen flickered. Then a picture appeared. There was Willis and the other hands entering the first chamber of the cliff dwelling. The images were surprisingly clear. The faces were recognizable. Elaine leaned forward tensely. She gave Rob a startled glance as he appeared on the screen.

On the film Elaine stepped through the entrance into the chamber. A gasp came from her. She glared over at him.

Rob let the film run. At last it showed Elaine leaving the chamber through the main entrance. Rob shut off the VCR.

"So what is this all about, Tyrell?" Elaine said in a cold voice. "Blackmail?"

"No, I'm working for the Governor's Task Force on Crime," he answered. "I was sent here to find out who was looting the cliff dwelling of artifacts. I must confess that you had me fooled, Elaine. I would have sworn that your father was behind it."

"My father!" She made a spitting noise. "Daddy couldn't steal pennies from a dead man's eyes! He can't even run a ranch profitably. That's why I decided to loot the dwelling. I need the money to save the ranch."

"Don't tell the scumbag any more, Elaine," said a voice behind the couch.

Rob turned his head to see Bert Willis standing behind him. He had a gun aimed at Rob's head.

Rob said, "I don't think you need a gun, Bert."

"I think we do, Tyrell. Or whatever your name is,"

Willis said grimly. "What now, Elaine?"

Elaine got to her feet. "First, we take this guy out to the cliff and make him show us the camera. We get rid of it."

Rob said quickly, "I have made a copy of the tape and mailed it to my supervisor."

Elaine smiled unpleasantly. "All that tape shows is me in something that looks like a cave. Without your testimony as to where it was taken, the cops have nothing."

Willis waved the gun. "And you're not going to be around to testify, Tyrell."

Rob felt the icy touch of fear. He'd been a fool. Storming in here without backup had been a bad mistake. Hard as it was to believe, he knew they were going to kill him.

"You can't be serious!" he said. "All you'll be charged with is a felony. You'd kill me over that?"

"What's at stake here," Elaine said, "is this ranch. If I don't get the money from the sale of the rest of those artifacts, the ranch goes. I was born and raised here. Shadow Ranch is my life. Whatever I have to do to save the ranch, I'll do."

Willis waved the gun again. "Let's go, hotshot. And don't try anything. If I have to kill you here and now, I will."

They walked outside the house. Willis was right behind Rob. The snout of the gun poked him in the back. The foreman's jacket hid the gun from anyone who might be watching. Once outside, Rob sent a quick look around. There was no one watching. The Acunas were gone from the picnic table. Rob remembered now hearing the cowbell clang while he was showing the film to Elaine. All the hands were having supper.

He could expect no help from any of the men.

Parked immediately in front of the house was a brand new, black pickup. The pickup had a double cab. Rob was directed to the front passenger seat. Elaine got into the back. Willis handed her the gun. She leaned across the seat. The gun barrel was cold against Rob's neck.

Willis got behind the wheel and drove away. Rob was seldom given to despair. But he felt despair now. They were going to kill him. And it was his own fault for being so stupid.

He turned his face toward Willis. "I think you're being foolish. There's no reason to kill me."

Without speaking Willis lashed out. He struck Rob across the mouth with the back of his hand. Rob's mouth filled with the coppery taste of his own blood. Suddenly all his fear was gone. He was filled with roaring rage. He would get out of this some way. Bert Willis was going to pay for hitting him.

The sun was almost down when they reached the cliff. Shadows fell across the entrance to the cliff chambers. Rob was directed inside first. Willis now had the gun.

Willis snapped, "Get the camera and be quick about it!"

Rob walked over to the far wall. His thoughts were racing. He knew that he only had minutes to live. On the way here he had looked for an opportunity to escape. There had been none. Neither Willis nor Elaine had relaxed for a second. He scraped away the dried mud around the camera. Then he took it out and started back across the room.

A few feet from where Willis stood, Rob noticed that the room had darkened. A muffled scream came from Elaine. Rob shot a glance at the entrance. A strange figure stood in the doorway. It had a round head and a body painted as a skeleton. Masau!

Elaine's scream had caused Willis to look around. Now he started to look back at Rob. He was too late. Rob had already launched himself. He drove into Willis chest high. They fell to the ground with Rob on top. The pistol fell out of the foreman's hand. It slid away out of reach.

The fall had dazed Willis. Rob sat astride him. He drove his fist into Willis' face again and again. His anger was driven by the humiliation of the past two hours. Finally he realized that the foreman was out cold.

Rob remembered Elaine and got quickly to his feet. But she posed no threat. She was held firmly by Masau. Dan Acuna stood behind her. He was lashing her hands together behind her back.

Rob took a step toward them. "Dan! How did—?" He stopped to stare at Masau who had taken off his mask. "You're not Masau! You're Will!"

For the first time since Rob had known him, Will Acuna smiled. "Give the man a silver dollar."

"But why?"

It was Dan who answered. "We learned about the cliff dwelling being looted. We got jobs on the ranch, hoping we could put a stop to it. We found the site, and I took one of the pots for evidence. Uncle decided to make himself up like Masau."

"It was Nephew's idea," Will interrupted. "He thought my popping up as Masau might scare the workers off. Unfortunately, it didn't work."

He shook his head. "We feel terrible about the man who fell. We didn't intend for anyone to get hurt."

Rob nodded. "That doesn't seem to be entirely your fault. If he hadn't panicked and Willis hadn't tried to stop him . . . It was you who pushed me into the pit, then pulled me out, wasn't it?"

Will nodded. "We liked you. I hoped to frighten you off. It didn't work. You're a stubborn man, Bobby."

"My name's not Bobby. It's Rob. Rob Harding. I'm working undercover. There were rumors about someone finding an Indian cliff dwelling and looting it."

"I figured you were more than you seemed to be," Dan said.

Rob said, "You guys were the ones who saved us from the flash flood."

Dan nodded. "Yeah. We didn't want you dead, even if you were the bad guys."

"And now you've saved me again."

Will Acuna said, "We saw you charge into the main house, dark as a thundercloud. Then from the cookhouse, we saw you leave with Willis and Miss Mackey."

"And that didn't smell or look right," Dan broke in. "So we followed you out here."

"I had planted a video camera in here to record who came and went." Rob pointed to the camera on the ground. It had fallen when he attacked Willis. "To my surprise it caught Elaine on film. I now know that she is behind the looting."

He looked at Elaine. She stared at him with bitter hatred.

Dan said, "I'm surprised, but not very much."

"Now I have to find a phone and get somebody out here," Rob said. "Could you guys watch over this pair until I get back?"

"Sure, no problem. But you don't need to drive anywhere. Use my cell phone." Dan took a cellular phone out his jacket pocket. "You'll probably have to go outside to get through. Meanwhile, I'll finish tying up Miss Mackey."

Rob took the phone. He laughed heartily. "I guess any good investigator should have one of these."

He stepped outside. Although the sun was down now, it was still daylight. He walked to the edge of the cliff before making the call. There was no point in calling Morgan's office. He called the sheriff's department. He quickly briefed them. They promised to send deputies to the site at once.

As he punched off the phone, Rob looked up at the top of the cliff. There, outlined in the fading light, stood the figure of Masau. The Hopi god had his arms raised high. He seemed to be staring directly into Rob's eyes.

Rob blinked. And the figure was gone. Was it a trick of light? Or had he imagined seeing Masau?

He started toward the entrance to call to Will Acuna. No, he wasn't going to tell them he had just seen their god on top of the cliff. They would probably think he was crazy.

No, this he would keep to himself. He laughed aloud and entered the cliff dwelling.